Samuel Wightman Culver

Crowned and Discrowned

Or the Rebel King and the Prophet of Ramah

Samuel Wightman Culver

Crowned and Discrowned
Or the Rebel King and the Prophet of Ramah

ISBN/EAN: 9783337273019

Printed in Europe, USA, Canada, Australia, Japan

Cover: Foto ©Andreas Hilbeck / pixelio.de

More available books at **www.hansebooks.com**

CROWNED AND DISCROWNED;

OR,

THE REBEL KING

AND

THE PROPHET OF RAMAH.

BY

REV. S. W. CULVER, A.M.

With an Introduction,

BY REV. G. W. EATON, D.D.,

PRES. OF THE THEOLOGICAL DEPARTMENT OF MADISON UNIVERSITY.

BOSTON:

GOULD AND LINCOLN,

59 WASHINGTON STREET.

NEW YORK: SHELDON AND COMPANY.

1870.

PREFACE.

THE following work is an attempt to realize
in a single instance the use that may
profitably be made of Old Testament narrative, when viewed in the light of history and from the position of Christian
enlightenment. The author has not called in the
aid of fiction to embellish the narrative; but it
is believed that in this case the truth itself
possesses an interest surpassing that of any
fiction. While, therefore, inspiration is permitted
to tell its own "unvarnished tale," the practical
Christian lessons educed are such as flow in
natural order of sequence from the narrative
itself.

The life of Saul, the rebel king, and his converse with Samuel, the prophet of Ramah, form
the groundwork of the volume. A series of

iii

incidents of thrilling interest, commencing with his inauguration and ending with his tragic death, are cited as illustrative and confirmatory of important spiritual lessons of practical and perpetual application.

If the work find interested readers, and if it have the effect in any measure to resolve perplexities, to encourage faith, to establish the wavering; or if any are led to see more clearly the dangers of disobedience, and so are impelled to betake themselves to the way of the divine testimony, the fondest hopes of the writer will be realized.

With a prayer that the divine blessing may rest upon it, and that it may go forth upon a mission of usefulness, it is committed to the publishers and the public by

THE AUTHOR.

CONTENTS.

CHAPTER II.

DEFECTIVE OBEDIENCE 43

CHAPTER III.

CHAPTER IV.

CHAPTER V.

INTRODUCTORY NOTE.

I HAVE perused in manuscript the pages of the following work. It is a valuable contribution to our religious and evangelical literature. In matter and style it possesses merits which should secure for it a wide circulation and general perusal among thoughtful and earnest Christians.

From suggestive passages in the life of Saul, the first king of Israel, the author has drawn a series of lessons of the highest practical moment; and of special application to the present as well as to the past. Indeed, a prominent excellence of the whole discussion consists in the discrimination, pertinence, and force, with which the

lessons deduced are applied to existing evils
and pernicious tendencies in Christian commu-
nities; and hence the work is of present and
urgent interest.

Under the heads of "Saul among the Prophets," "Defective Obedience," "The Rebel-
lious Sacrifice," "A Proverb in Israel," and
"Fruitless Supplication," various radical questions, bearing on religious opinions and life, are
discussed with a force of logic and appositeness
of illustration, which cannot fail to render valuable
and efficient aid in relieving the perplexities of
believers in the Bible as a revelation from God,
and in answering the captious cavils of the
sceptic.   With unflinching fidelity, thoroughness,
and loyalty to God and his truth, the author
has set forth the fundamental principles of
Christian ethics, or gospel morality; and the
spirit and temper with which they should be carried out in practice. Unquestioning, unreserved,
and cordial obedience to the plain commands of

God is clearly and impressively shown to be the prime and exclusive element in all acceptable service to Him, as our only Sovereign. The animadversions upon Episcopacy and Infant Baptism will, of course, be more acceptable and edifying to Baptists than to the adherents of these forms; but the principles and tests applied to these cases of aberration from revealed truth cannot be gainsaid by any sincere and earnest Christian, of whatever name. Their practical application can alone furnish grounds of difference of opinion and practice. These principles and tests, logically and scripturally carried out, as the author has done, necessitate his conclusions.

The style of the author is singularly perspicuous, direct, and free from ambitious rhetorical ornament; but it rises at times to a high order of eloquence and beauty. The spirit and tone of the whole work is eminently evangelical, earnest and solemn, and well suited to the grave and high themes discussed. The conclusion contains a powerful and pungent appeal, especially to the young, in application of the subjects which have passed under consideration.

G. W. EATON.

HAMILTON, N. Y., March, 1870.

I.

SAUL AMONG THE PROPHETS.

CROWNED AND DISCROWNED.

CHAPTER I.

SAUL AMONG THE PROPHETS.

I.

THE RELATIVE FUNCTIONS OF PROPHET AND KING IN ISRAEL.

SAMUEL, the first in the line of the prophets, and Saul, the first in the line of the
kings of Israel, are the characters that
especially claim our attention in the first
book of Samuel. It was a new era in
the history of the nation when the kingly and
prophetic functions became permanently sepa-
rated. The government had been established
as a pure theocracy. The mediator, who was
its divinely appointed head, sustained to the
people the relation of religious teacher and
temporal ruler; combining thus in one the
prophet and the king. It was the design that

the human administration should always be associated with the divine counsel and guidance. The earthly ruler was always to hold himself in subordination to the divine ruler; the lower to follow, implicitly, the enactments of the higher law.

In this respect it was a type of what any government must be that would possess the elements of stability and permanence. The government of God must constantly be owned and obeyed, as supreme. When the divine ruler is forgotten, and the merely human is invested with the attributes that belong only to him, disaster and misery, if not speedy destruction, are sure to follow. The tendency which was now maturing among the people of Israel was one that is common among men; namely, to clothe human government, whether it be that of many or of one, whether it be that of an autocracy or a democracy, with irresponsible power.

II.

THE REVOLUTION.

The first book of Samuel records his call to the prophetic office and his administration of

the government while he judged Israel. In his
old age he appointed his sons judges in his
stead. "The corrupt administration of justice
by Samuel's sons furnished the occasion to the
people for rejecting that theocracy, of which
they neither appreciated the value, nor, through
their unfaithfulness to it, enjoyed the full advantages. An invasion by the Amorites seems
also to have conspired with the cause just mentioned, and with the love of novelty, in prompt-
ing the demand for a king,— an officer evidently alien to the genius of the theocracy, though
contemplated as a historical certainty, and pro-
vided for by the Jewish lawgiver."

The account of this revolution is given in the
following words: "Then all the elders of Israel gathered themselves together, and came to
Samuel, to Ramah; and said unto him, Behold
thou art old, and thy sons walk not in thy ways:
now make us a king to judge us, like all the nations. But the thing displeased Samuel, when
they said Give us a king. And Samuel prayed
unto the Lord. And the Lord said unto Samuel, Hearken unto the voice of the people, in
all that they say unto thee; for they have not

rejected thee, but they have rejected me, that I
should not reign over them."

III.

THE CALLING OF THE KING.

Finding himself a guest of the prophet under
circumstances which, one would think, could
have little to do with the establishment of a
kingdom, Saul is surprised with the announce-
ment that he is to be king over Israel. With
undissembled diffidence and self-distrust, the
youth shrinks from so great an honor and responsibility. He is, nevertheless, encouraged
by the aged prophet, who, the next morning,
anoints him king. He then assures him, that,
as he comes to the hill of God, and meets the
company of the prophets coming down from
thence, the Spirit of the Lord will come upon
him, and he shall prophesy; and shall be turned
into another man.

The sequel is thus described: "And it was so
when he had turned his back to go from Samuel,
God gave him another heart; and all these
signs came to pass that day; and when they

came thither to the hill, behold, the prophets met him, and the Spirit of God came upon him, and he prophesied among them. And it came to pass, when all that knew him beforetime saw that, behold, he prophesied among the prophets, then the people said one to another, 'What is this that is come to the son of Kish? Is Saul also among the prophets?"

The spirit of prophecy was bestowed upon him as a fitting preparation for the proper exercise of the kingly function; as essential, in fact, to the right administration of the government. It is worthy of notice, how, in this whole account, the prophet takes precedence of the king, the religious teacher of the incumbent of the highest political office, the word of God of the exercise of arbitrary power. This is the order of precedence that God has established for all time. Only wicked legislators and corrupt politicians ever seek to reverse it. And the fact that, in any case, the attempt is made to reverse it, is an unmistakable mark of their wickedness and corruption.

IV.

THE INQUIRY OF THE PEOPLE AND THE IMPORTANT QUESTION.

The question, "Is Saul also among the prophets?" it will be seen, is not so much an interrogation as it is an expression of wonder at the strange event that had come to the son of Kish. What, then, we are led to inquire, was the ground of their astonishment? Not, surely, that a fellow-being had suddenly been endued with the gift of inspiration and received the prophetic afflatus. The prophetic had been a co-ordinate part of their own history as a nation. The name of the aged prophet who had judged Israel so long must have become familiar to them as a household word. Besides, there was the school of the prophets, under his tuition. It was a company of these that Saul met, when the Spirit of God came upon him, and he prophesied.

The astonishment of the people may have arisen from the same cause as that of Saul himself when Samuel told him that he was to be king; namely, his own obscurity and that of his family. On that memorable occasion he is said to have answered, "Am not I a Benjamite, of the smallest of the tribes of Israel? and my family the least of all the families of the tribe of Benjamin? Wherefore, then, speakest thou so to me?"

There was that, too, in the character of Saul, that gave little promise of royal dignity and elevation. He seems to have been naturally timid and shrinking, as the incident just mentioned indicates. Another incident places this characteristic in still more striking light. When the day of his inauguration came, and the sacred lot, as it was given forth, fell, first upon the tribe of Benjamin, and then upon the family of Matri, and finally upon Saul the son of Kish, the prospective monarch could nowhere be found. "Therefore," it is said, "they inquired of the Lord further, if the man should yet come thither; and the Lord answered, 'Behold, he hath hidden himself among the stuff.'" That such a youth should suddenly lose all his timidity, and stand forth boldly and prophesy among the prophets, was, surely, not a little remarkable.

Marvellous as it seemed that Saul should ap-

pear among the prophets, the people were
nevertheless right glad to receive him as their
sovereign, when he was at length brought forth
from his hiding-place and stood among them.
And it is not a little interesting to notice on
what ground they predicated their estimate of
him. It. shows how little they were prepared
to appreciate moral excellence and spiritual
greatness ; how much they had fallen under the
dominion of the senses. It was noticed that he
was higher than any of the people from his·
shoulders and upward. As if greatness of stature were any index of greatness of soul. As if
weight of muscle were indicative of weight of
intellect, or character and executive ability
were to be estimated in pounds avoirdupois.
Nevertheless, height of stature seems to have
been the thing that specially impressed the people, and determined their choice. "And all the
people shouted, and said, God save the king."

V.

MORAL INCONGRUITIES.

The question, "Is Saul also among the prophets?" is one that we are inclined to raise for

another reason. We know that Saul was a bad man. It was doubtless in allusion to him that it was said, " I gave them a king in mine anger, and took him away in my wrath." When the people clamored for a king to be appointed them, it was foretold what should be the character of his reign. It was described as an unmitigated tyranny. That description concluded, " And ye shall cry out in that day because of your king which ye shall have chosen you, and the Lord will not hear you in that day." Only a wicked prince could have fulfilled this prophecy. We know that Saul did fulfil it to the very letter. We know that he was characteristically jealous and sullen, melancholy and misanthropic, and that he became more and more unscrupulous and tyrannical till death closed his guilty career. It is the moral incongruity between such a character and the holiness that we feel belongs to the spirit of inspiration, that awakens our astonishment that they could have been brought into such intimate conjunction; that a man who became so badly eminent should have been even temporarily inspired of God. It is in view of this' incongruity that we are impelled to exclaim, "Is Saul also among the prophets?"

But Saul does not stand alone in this ambiguous position. Balaam, the son of Besor, who loved the wages of unrighteousness, and whose whole course, both before and afterwards, was in open contradiction to goodness and rectitude, was, nevertheless, temporarily inspired. Nor do we forget that among the disciples first sent forth by our Saviour to preach the gospel, and furnished for the occasion with such gifts as inspiration only could bestow, was Judas, one of the twelve, who also betrayed him. These lives, so darkened by sin, were for brief intervals illuminated with the holiest light. Though their ordinary course was that of evil, waxing worse and worse, they were for a time, it would seem, brought by the power of God into conformity with goodness and truth.

But we must remark, in regard to them, that though they were manifestly among the prophets, and undoubtedly spake by inspiration, such are not the characters that have been made the vehicles for the establishment of any part of the ground-work of our faith. That "sure word of prophecy" to which we "do well that we take heed," was uttered by "holy men, who spake as they were moved by the Holy Ghost." God has chosen for the purpose of conveying His lively oracles to our race only such as were in harmony with the work to which they were called.

If the spirit of inspiration has sometimes fallen upon evil men, overmastering them as a divine possession, and counterworking their evil for a time, this, so far from weakening our confidence in the mission of prophets and apostles, rather tends to confirm it, by showing how little the evil that is in the world is able to resist the spirit that is in them. How possible it is that an evil agent may be pressed into the service of God, and made to work obediently against his most cherished purposes. In short, how much greater is He who is in the true prophet than he that is in the world.

VI.

NEED OF MORAL DISCRIMINATION.

We need to make a very broad distinction between the truth and its advocates; between a good cause and the agents by whom it is sought to be promoted; between beneficent institutions and those who may be for a time identified with them. If a liar speaks the truth, is it, thereby, rendered any less true? If habitual parsimony is, on some special occasion, moved with a generous impulse, is benevolence rendered any less commendable? If a son of perdition lends his efforts to the promotion of a righteous cause, is it therefore any less righteous? Surely not. And this single consideration is sufficient to silence the whole of that hostile casuistry in which Christianity and the Christian church are made to bear the odium of all the ungodly characters and evil practices that shelter themselves under the Christian name. We would not be understood as offering any apology for such inconsistencies. What we insist upon is, that they militate not in the least against the sacredness of the cause, or the excellence of the institutions with which they may, for the time, be connected. The cause must stand upon its own merits, and they upon theirs. We take it that when one is habitually extortionate, if his word is not to be depended on in the transactions of business, or if he be an evil speaker, impure in conversation, irascible in temper, or a drunkard, or profane, these are indications, not to be mistaken, that grace is wanting. "How shall we that are dead to sin live any longer therein?" "By their fruits ye shall know them. Do men gather grapes of thorns, or figs of thistles?"

VII.

THE FALSE PROFESSOR.

Now we grant all that the casuist can consistently ask. We grant that there are false professors of religion in every Christian community; that there may be found members in any Christian church that are living blemishes on its fair fame. "Spots in your feasts of charity, when they feast with you, feeding themselves without fear." But when the opposer would hold forth these as fair representatives of the cause with which they for the time stand connected, we do not hesitate to say that the implication is not merely erroneous, it is positively and wickedly false. Nothing could give them such undue prominence but the glaring contrast that evidently subsists between the profession of such individuals and their practice. They are externally identified with the church, but not truly of it. They belong to the church, as barnacles belong to the ship; as excrescences, that mar its beauty and impede its progress. When the casuist is himself a disciple of a different faith, and points to the inconsistencies of professors for the purpose of bringing our evangelical faith into disrepute, we feel inclined to retort, " We thank God that every true church of Christ has character enough to make such connections appear inconsistent. It can bear the transient disgrace without material harm. Who, let me ask, ever knew of a society of Atheists, or Deists, or Universalists, or Spiritualists, being dishonored by the ungodliness and immoralities of its members?"

In the true church of Christ the evils are brought into special prominence; because they are relieved against "the pillar and ground of the truth" and the spotless purity of our evangelical faith. We wonder at the ambiguous position of the false professor, and are fain to exclaim with them of ancient time, "Is Saul also among the prophets?" But Saul among the prophets, or Judas among the apostles, makes nothing against the sacredness of prophecy on the one hand, or of the apostleship on the other. Nor do cases like these make in the least against the sacredness of the Christian cause, or the excellence of a truly godly and consistent church-membership.

VIII.

A CLASS OF CONSCIENTIOUS SCRUPLES CONSIDERED.

A class of conscientious scruples may also be met with the same consideration. It has been asked, Does not an individual, in becoming a member of a church, thereby endorse the character of all its members? And here, while we would offer no apology for a neglect of discipline, that often may become an occasion for unfavorable criticism, we unhesitatingly reply that he does not. He has thereby endorsed the character of no individual on earth, not even his own. What he has endorsed is the great principle for the sake of which the church exists, and the divine purpose she was designed to subserve. He has endorsed that which gives to the organization vitality and significance,— the One Lord, One Faith, and One Baptism.

And in so doing he has offered the strongest possible protest against ungodliness and immorality, wherever they may exist. He has. professed his faith in a holiness so transcendent, that it is required, in every single case, that he should be "washed with the washing of regeneration and the renewing of the Holy Spirit." Is Isaiah, let us ask, responsible for the character of Saul? Is John responsible for that of Judas? So neither is the honest and consistent member of a Christian church responsible for the character of the false professor who may, temporarily, be associated with him. But let us not fail to notice, in this connection, how strongly every one who has named the name of Christ is admonished to depart from all iniquity; to shun the very appearance of evil; to live soberly, righteously, and godly, in this present evil world, that we give none occasion to the adversary to speak reproachfully.

IX.

DISCRIMINATION IN THE CASE OF MINISTERIAL APOSTASY.

Still more strongly is an application of our subject suggested to another, but co-ordinate, topic; I mean ministerial apostasy. There have been men who have, for a time, been eminently successful in the work of the Christian ministry; whose labors have resulted in bringing multitudes to the knowledge of the truth; who not only preached, but administered the ordinances of the gospel with great acceptance, — who have subsequently fallen from this eminence of usefulness, and have proved themselves unworthy of the Christian name; and, in some instances, they have passed directly over to an equal eminence in infamy. The questions which very naturally occur in such cases are, Are conversions under such a ministry genuine? And are the ordinances administered by them valid?

Only distinguish between the truth and its advocates, and the answer is clear. The truth is the instrument to which belongs converting

3

grace. The Holy Spirit is the agent by whom it is wielded. The change that we call conversion is, therefore, divinely wrought. It is the divine, not the human, agent that gives character to it. The human is but the vehicle by which the truth is brought in contact with the understanding. Further than this, it sinks into absolute nothingness. " Who," asks the apostle, " who is Paul, or who is Apollos, but ministers by whom ye believed? Paul planted, Apollos watered ; but God gave the increase." " The excellency of the power," he continues, "is of God and not of us." If, then, the work is divinely wrought, the subsequent apostasy, or even the present insincerity of the human agent cannot affect its genuineness. " Some, indeed," says Paul, in his epistle to the Philippians, " preach Christ even of envy and strife, and some also of good-will. The one preach Christ of contention, not sincerely, supposing to add affliction to my bonds ; but the other of love, knowing that I am set for the defence of the gospel. What then? Notwithstanding, every way, whether in pretence or in truth, Christ is preached; and I therein do rejoice, yea, and will rejoice."

X.

DISCRIMINATION AS TO THE ORDINANCES.

Again, as to the validity of the ordinances; this must depend upon two conditions. The first is, whether the observance be really of Christ's appointment. That cannot be a Christian ordinance that has not been established by the express authority of Christ. The first question to ask, then, in regard to any observance purporting to be Christian, is, does it bear, clear and unmistakably, the image and superscription of the great Head of the Church? If it cannot show this proof it is invalid, however smuggled into general acceptance. By no art ecclesiastic can a mere human invention, however reverently observed, whatever circumstances of solemnity may be thrown around it, be lifted to the position and stamped with the seal of genuineness.

The second condition concerns the candidate himself. It is, that he have faith. "Without faith it is impossible to please God." "Whatsoever is not of faith is sin." Indeed, without faith it would not be an act of obedience to Christ at all. It must be as obvious as any truism can be that a Christian faith is essential to the right observance of a Christian ordinance. It is a transaction between the believer and his Saviour, by means of which he holds communion with him, and receives grace from him. The administrator's place is entirely subordinate. The validity of Christian ordinances, as well as the genuineness of conversion, rests on the Divine agency present rather than the human.

Let us only distinguish properly between the truth and its advocates, between Christian institutions and those who may, temporarily, be identified with them, and our deepest questionings are forthwith resolved. The human, the transient, the perishable, passes away; but the Divine, the Spiritual, the Eternal, remains yesterday, to-day, and forever. Our faith must stand, not in the wisdom of men, but in the power of God. Though Saul was among the prophets, and Judas was among the apostles, there yet remains "the foundation of apostles and prophets, Jesus Christ himself being the chief corner-stone." And "Other foundation can no man lay than that is laid."

Though there should be found within the pale of the Christian Church, and even among those with whom we have taken sweet counsel and in whose company we have often walked to the house of God, those who shall fall away, or those who turn the grace of God into lasciviousness, even denying the Lord that bought them; yet amid all individual changes that Church remains "the pillar and ground of the truth," the purchase of a Saviour's blood, the light of the world, holding forth the Word of Life to a race rapidly hastening to eternal death, crowned with the glory of a completed redemption, " her walls Salvation and her gates Praise." And though in the ranks of the Christian ministry apostates multiply, till the true disciples are wont to exclaim, "Alas! that these Sauls should ever have been among the prophets!" nevertheless, that ministry exists by the appointment of Christ, and with it remains the promise of the risen Saviour: "Lo! I am with you always, even to the end of the world."

XI.

FAITH MUST STAND NOT IN THE FALLIBLE, BUT IN THE INFALLIBLE.

God only is unchangeable. Changefulness is an attribute of man. There is a mournful possibility lying in the way of every individual. Humanly speaking, none of us can tell what moral position he may occupy in the coming years. If an apostle, gifted with the highest inspiration, after having been caught up to the third heaven, and there hearing words unutterable, and beholding ineffable glories, felt it necessary to strive, lest, having preached to others, he himself should be a cast-away, it surely does not become us to be self-confident. For aught you know, dear reader, he who has preached the gospel to you with much assurance; who has buried you in baptism, in your obedience to Christ; from whose hands you have received the symbols of a Saviour's dying love; whose timely word of admonition has made you braver, truer, nobler, stronger, in all spiritual grace and strength; warned you in the hour of danger, counselled you in your darkness, consoled you in your sorrow, encouraged you in your despondency, and contributed in numberless ways to your growth in grace, — may end his days in utter ungodliness, a wrecked and ruined apostate.

We shrink with instinctive horror from such a result. Nevertheless it is a possibility, — a possibility not to be set aside, while the perilous gift of free agency remains. But that possibility should teach us how needful it is that our faith should learn to stand alone, — how needful it is that we look steadfastly beyond the poor, and weak, and fallible human instrumentality to the divine Being, who never disappoints the confidence that rests in His Eternal Power and Godhead; according to whose eternal purpose, and in whose hand, the instrumental agency has been used. In short, how important it is that our faith be rooted and grounded in eternal verities. Moreover, let us observe how it becomes us to watch and pray, that we enter not into temptation; that we pray with all prayer, and watch thereunto with untiring vigilance, that we may be kept by the power of God, through faith, unto salvation.

II.

DEFECTIVE OBEDIENCE.

CHAPTER II.

I.

SAUL'S DISOBEDIENCE AND THE PROPHET'S REBUKE.

THE fifteenth chapter of the first Book
of Samuel records a portion of Old Testament history of peculiar interest in
itself, and of additional interest because
of the use that has been made of it in
the casuistry of the caviller. In the first verses
of this chapter the prophet is represented as ad-
dressing Saul, king of Israel, in these words:
" The Lord sent me to anoint thee to be king
over his people, over Israel : now hearken thou
unto the voice of the words of the Lord. Thus
saith the Lord of Hosts ; I remember that which
Amalek did to Israel, how he laid wait for him
by the way when he came up from Egypt.
Now go and smite Amalek, and utterly destroy
all that they have, and spare them not, but slay

both man and woman, infant and suckling, camel and ass."

Saul accepts the commission, and, at the head of an army of two hundred thousand men and ten thousand men of Judah, goes forth to the work of extermination. Separating the Kenites from the Amalekites, because they had showed kindness to Israel when they came out of Egypt, the doomed race are smitten from Havilah to Shur. But so far from carrying out fully the edict of destruction, Saul and the people spared Agag and the best of the spoil, and of the oxen and of the fatlings, and of the lambs, and all that was good; but everything that was vile and refuse, that they destroyed utterly.

It is hardly possible to ascribe this conduct of Saul, in sparing Amalek, to any more worthy motive than a vain desire to have the captive king to grace the triumph which he felt sure he was to enjoy when he came into his own land. Nor can we suppose that any higher motive than covetousness prompted him to spare the best of the spoil. At all events, it was certain he had not fulfilled his commission. He was sent forth on a mission of chastisement;

he had returned with the booty of a plunderer.
Saul must have felt that he was now occupying
quite an equivocal position. He had not been
on terms of mutual confidence with the prophet for some time before; for this was not the
first time that Saul had failed to obey the voice
of the Lord. There was little reason for him
to think that he would now be received into
confidence.

In the mean time, it had been told to Samuel,
"Saul came to Carmel, and, behold, he set him
up a place, and is gone about, and is passed on,
and is gone down to Gilgal." All this, probably, to avoid, or at least delay, the expected
and dreaded meeting. But avoidance is impossible. Samuel, it is said, comes to Saul; and
Saul, assuming the airs of undoubting confidence and conscious rectitude, meets the prophet with the joyful exclamation, "Blessed art
thou of the Lord! I have performed the word
of the Lord." Imagine, if possible, the look of
calm majesty and keen rebuke which the prophet turns upon the trembling king as he in-
quires, "What meaneth then this bleating of the
sheep in my ears, and this lowing of the oxen

which I hear?" But Saul was not wanting in resources for such an occasion. When, indeed, was ever a guilty man wanting in expedients to hide his guilt? It was the people, he declares, who had spared the best of the spoil. As if the people could have done it without their leader's consent and complicity. But he further affirms the purpose to have been an entirely honorable one. They have spared this spoil, he tells the prophet, " to sacrifice unto the Lord thy God." As if such an oblation could, by any possibility, be accepted.

He has no opportunity to offer reasons for the sparing of Agag before the prophet's voice arrests him once more. And Samuel said, " Hath the Lord as great delight in burnt-offerings and sacrifices, as in obeying the voice of the Lord? Behold, to obey is better than sacrifice, and to hearken than the fat of rams. For disobedience is as the sin of witchcraft, and stubbornness is as iniquity and idolatry. Because thou hast rejected the word of the Lord, he hath also rejected thee from being king." The sequel is told in the following words : "Then said Samuel, bring ye hither to me

Agag, the king of the Amalekites. And Agag came unto him delicately. And Agag said, Surely, the bitterness of death is past. And Samuel said, As thy sword hath made women childless, so shall thy mother be childless among women. And Samuel hewed Agag in pieces, before the Lord, in Gilgal. Then Samuel went to Ramah, and Saul went up to his own house, in Gibeah of Saul. And Samuel came no more to see Saul unto the day of his death : nevertheless Samuel mourned for Saul, and the Lord repented that he had made Saul king over Israel."

II.

SCEPTICAL CAVILS.

Scepticism has persistently used this account for a very different purpose from that of enforcing the lesson which it teaches. It has been pressed into service for the purpose of making out the charge of cruelty against the Hebrews, and by consequence against the God of the Hebrews. It is enough for the corroboration of a Christian faith, that the credibility and inspiration of the Scriptures do not rest on our ability to vindicate the ways of God to man, in every case. His ways, it must be admitted, are not our ways, or his thoughts our thoughts. He judges from a loftier view than any we are competent to take, from a higher wisdom than any we can fully comprehend. There are mysteries in his providential dealings that we cannot explain, and so there are in his judicial government. Do we charge the Creator with cruelty because of the ravages of earthquakes, fires, and floods? Shall we then arraign, and try by our limited standards, the putting forth of some act of that Creator's retributive justice? It were surely wiser far to admit that there are heights in the divine purposes which our highest wisdom cannot reach, and depths in the divine counsels that our sounding-lines cannot fathom.

But a partial explanation, in this case, one which is sufficient to parry the force of hostile criticism, is to be found in the fact that the Amalekites were the bitter, unrelenting, and cruel foes of Israel; from generation to generation persistently seeking their destruction. Without the least provocation, they came from their land, on the southern border of Canaan, to attack the Israelites in the wilderness. Defeated in a most sanguinary battle, they returned to their own land, but with the purpose ever cherished to frustrate the purpose of God in the peaceful establishment of Israel in the promised land. They made frequent raids upon the borders of Israel, and, in the days of the judges, joined with their enemies, the Midianites, to make war upon them. To defeat the purpose of God in the settlement of his people, and thus to defeat his purposes of mercy to our guilty race, — this was the ungracious task which Amalek had undertaken. God had now borne with them till the cup of their iniquities was full, and therefore determined to blot out the name of Amalek from under heaven.

But why this summary slaughter of Agag, after he had been disarmed, and when he was held a powerless and therefore harmless captive? Undoubtedly Agag had been a most cruel and bloodthirsty prince. As much is indicated in the language of the prophet : " As thy sword hath made women childless, so shall

4

thy mother be childless among women." His
cruelty, his perfidy, his inhumanity, and his
high-handed rebellion against the laws both
of God and man, are sufficient to justify the
judgments that made his life the forfeit of his
crimes. It is neither wise, nor politic, nor
humane, nor merciful, nor just, that the chief
of a great rebellion should go unpunished.
Suffice it to say that Saul's commission, besides having the authority of God, had every
corroborative circumstance that reason could
presume to ask. His disobedience, and the
prophet's reproof, serve to enforce this one
important lesson : "Behold, to obey is better
than sacrifice."

III.

THE LESSON CONSIDERED.

This lesson, so rigorously applied in this
particular case, has all the characteristics of
a general principle ; and, therefore, finds as
ready and forcible an application in every other
case that can occur in the history of the human
race. Where God's will is known, the only
position at all consistent for a rational creature

is that of unquestioning, uncompromising submission. Where his command is given, we
may not think to alter, to abridge, or supplement that command. Our duty is simple :
that of full, unreserved, undeviating obedience.
This lesson is enforced, in the history of Saul,
rather negatively than positively. The positive
side is seen in the first prayer offered by Saul
of Tarsus : "Lord, what wilt thou have me
to do?"

Saul's first error, it will be seen, was that of
defect. He had commenced the work assigned
him, and carried it forward successfully. But
he had failed to complete what he had begun.
He rebelled, not in what he had done, but in
what he had left undone, in that he turned
from the divine command to his own wisdom,
and stayed his hand too soon. This error
wrought all his subsequent disasters, lost for
him and his posterity the throne of Israel, and
brought him finally to a violent death.

Bear in mind the strong terms in which our
Saviour and the apostles urge upon us this
lesson of obedience : "No man, having put
his hand to the plough, and looking back, is fit

for the kingdom of God." "He that taketh not his cross, and followeth after me, is not worthy of me." These passages place before us, in most striking light, the dangers of defective obedience. Indeed, where the authority is plainly revealed, pointing out a plain path for us to follow, and we turn aside from that path, we place ourselves in active rebellion against him; and thereby renounce all title to that rich inheritance of blessings purchased for us by a Saviour's precious blood, and which, though solely the gift of divine grace, can nevertheless be received only in the line of obedience. The law of the kingdom of grace the apostle announces to be this: "To those who, by patient continuance in well-doing, seek for glory, honor, immortality, Eternal Life." How urgently does he press upon the early Christians the importance of a close, practical adherence to the word of God! expressing his astonishment that any should swerve from it, and his doubt of such as have turned aside unto another gospel, and declaring "though we, or an angel from heaven, preach any other gospel unto you than that we have preached, let him be accursed."

IV.

ILLUSTRATED IN THE HISTORY OF THE CHRISTIAN CHURCH.

But for the failure to comply with the command of Christ and the counsel of the apostles, how different a history might have been that of the Christian Church! Her whole course would have been a pathway of light and glory, and to-day she might stand forth in the beauty of holiness, like the woman clothed with the sun. But, alas! right under the eyes of the apostles, and in spite of all their vigilance, the disposition manifested itself to turn from the pure word of God, and render to him only a defective obedience. Thus early were visible the very evils that subsequently grew so rapidly into the greatness that resulted in the proud domination and enormous usurpations of the Man of Sin, and which plunged the Christian nations into that long night of ignorance and superstition know as the Dark Ages, — a period in which the true faith seemed buried under a more than heathen darkness and idolatry.

This tendency to leave incomplete the work which God assigns us, and turn from our Heavenly Guide to our merely human wisdom, — oh, it is the tendency of human nature ! It is the natural working of that perversity of the human heart that gives painful evidence of the prevalence of sin. How much of energy is lost to the cause of Christ by stopping to gather up the spoils, or to secure a triumph ! One can hardly read the history of any one of those great movements in the religious world called reformations, without mingling with emotions of joy that so much good was done feelings of deep regret that the work was left so incomplete.

V.

THE REFORMATIONS OF THE SIXTEENTH AND EIGHTEENTH CENTURIES.

Luther hurled the doctrine of justification by faith into the midst of Rome, with all the energy of his own great soul: a live coal, which he had taken, all glowing, from the altar of his God; and the new seed thus sown was bearing its fruit all over Europe, some thirty, some sixty, and some an hundred fold. But Luther could not consent to take *the Bible alone* as the standard both of his faith and practice; and so, abandoning the great Protestant principle, he stayed his hand, and left, still entire, in the churches that grew up under his labors, all the Roman Catholic observances and implements of superstition against which there had not been levelled some specific Scripture prohibition. The leaven of corruption thus left in these churches did not fail to bear its fruit in due season. Luther and his co-laborers also felt that they must organize this work, and give it shape and con-sistency, instead of leaving it to shape itself into the simple modes of the New Testament. They did organize it, accordingly, and made it intensely Lutheran. And the result was a Lutheran hierarchy that, in some instances, has developed a tyranny and corruption equal to that of the hierarchy of Rome itself.

In England, the real reformation was frowned upon by the dominant church, and has never been accepted by it. What the adherents of that church called the reformation was not worthy of the name. It accomplished scarcely more than to make the king the head of the church instead of the pope, and left the people only less burdened under the oppressive weight of the English Episcopacy than they had been under the papal rule.

In the great Methodist movement of the eighteenth century, Wesley and his coadjutors proclaimed, with a boldness and earnestness seldom if ever surpassed, the ruined condition of the sinner and the need of the new birth. And this doctrine they held forth as a flaming torch, in the midst of a cold, speculative, and half atheistic age. Against the sleek formalism of the times, they persistently asserted that without inward spiritual light, without religion in the soul, there was no religion at all, and no salvation. With these pure Scripture truths their own souls were on fire. Others soon caught the flame. In spite of jibes and jeers, in spite of ridicule and persecution, the influence of their preaching spread rapidly over the British Isles, and was borne by favoring gales across the seas; till, along our own shores,

and far into the depths of American wilds,
sounded forth the word with unwonted energy,
"Ye must be born again." All religious de-
nominations, in whom remained a spark of
true vitality, felt the quickening glow; converts
were multiplied as the drops of the morning.
Incalculable good was done. How great the
amount, it is impossible adequately to estimate;
nor can it be estimated, till the day when
Christ shall make up his jewels. And, since
so much good was done, it is with pain that we
are compelled to notice that an element of corruption was at work, in the very midst of it,
in a failure, in so many things, to adhere
strictly to the authority of the word of God.
Even the doctrine of inward spiritual light,
often left unguarded, was made the ultimate
test of religious experience, instead of itself
being subjected to the test of the written word,
and the religious enthusiast gave himself up
to inward impulses and supposed special reve-
lations, with all the self-devotion of the mystic.
The result has been a zeal not according to
knowledge, and a wild enthusiasm, that has
often manifested itself in noisy and disorderly

demonstrations. The doctrine was true. The error was, that the experience was not, in all cases, brought to the test of ultimate truth.

But the gravest error of all was, that Wesley, like Luther, felt that he must put this movement into leading-strings; like Saul, that he must gather up the spoil, and secure his own triumph. And so he proceeded to organize it, at the dictate of his own wisdom, without looking for authority to the word of God. The result was, a magnificent piece of ecclesiastical machinery, on which the inventor had so impressed his personal qualities that it is not too much to say that Wesley was, to the Methodist organization, instead of Christ; the whole pressed into subordination to his one will, and that one will the supreme law. There was a vast amount of genuine spiritual religion, but it was compelled to find its external development in forms and modes from which the authority of the Great Head of the church was completely excluded. That organization is felt to be more and more burdensome, and the call is, ever and anon, heard for revisions and modifications. But no changes will permanently avail that stop short of the acknowledgment of the Word of God as the only and sufficient rule, and the authority of God as the only authority, in matters of religion, both external and internal.

VI.

PREVALENT DEFECTS IN CHRISTIAN SERVICE.

We in this age are guilty of deficiencies; but our defects arise, for the most part, from a contrary source. We fail to find among us the glowing zeal and devoted energy to carry us onward to the fulness of the measure of Christian obedience. Our defects are not those of excess of strength, but of conscious weakness. We err with Joash, King of Israel, who, when told to take the arrow which Elisha had chosen as a prophetic symbol, and smite upon the earth, smote thrice, and stayed his hand; whereas he should have smitten five or six times: then should he have smitten Syria till he had consumed it; whereas now he could smite it but thrice. Who can doubt that there is urgent need that we put more of the energies that God has given us into our religious activities? A little of the service of God here and there, and at intervals only, while the best of our energies are given to worldly ends and selfish interests, — this is the common rule. We obey the voice of the Lord but partially, while we make sure of the best of the spoil; and our successes are therefore rendered proportionally less.

We enter upon the fulfilment of the divine command, but find ourselves discouraged and hindered by obstacles that, in any other line of action, would not have impeded our progress for a moment. We take the arrow of the Lord's deliverance and smite only thrice, whereas we should have smitten five or six times. Would to God that the indomitable energy of Luther, and the fiery zeal of Wesley and Whitfield, and the lofty ardor and godly earnestness of Edwards and the Tenants, pervaded both the ministry and membership of the churches of the present day! Would to God that all the Lord's people were prophets! Alas! our obedience to the divine commands is defective. Our imitation of Christ, our Great Exemplar, is defec-

tive; our interest in the salvation of souls is
defective; our labors for the advancement of
Christ's kingdom are defective; and must we
not own, with sorrow and shame, as the root of
innumerable evils, that our love to Christ is also defective? and where can we look, over the
whole field of our religious life, that we are not
compelled to witness the sad memorials of our
deficiencies? Oh, we need more of spiritual energy, the vital energy of faith; need to put
our activities into the hand of God, to be used
as instruments for the accomplishment of his
purposes. We need a greater holiness of aim
and consecration of purpose, that will make no
reservations for our selfishness; reserve no
gratifications for our pride; leave no occasion
for our indolence; but that shall destroy utterly our besetting sins, as the prophet hewed
Agag in pieces before the Lord.

We need more of vital godliness, more of the
power of religion; a clearer demonstration to
the world that the Gospel is the Power of God,
—the power of God unto salvation to every
one that believeth. Can we endure the test
which Elijah instituted before the prophets of

Baal? "The God that answereth by fire, let him be God." Dare we submit to this test before an unbelieving world? While the loftiest motives that we can possibly conceive urge us to faithfulness; while the infinite love and mighty sacrifice of Christ enforce the lesson of obedience; while Gethsemane pleads, and Calvary urges, and Heaven invites, are not our zeal and energy often outdone by those whose inspiration is brought only from earthly sources? We may rest assured, that, when our consecration is complete, and our obedience is full, God will accept the offering, and the fire from the upper sanctuary will come down and consume the sacrifice.

III.

THE REBELLIOUS SACRIFICE.

CHAPTER III.

THE REBELLIOUS SACRIFICE.

I.

A SECOND LESSON SUGGESTED.

HERE is yet another lesson, a totally different one from the preceding, but co-ordinate with it, which we need just as much to consider: namely, that we cannot supplement our defective obedience by any subsequent sacrifices.

When the prophet had blasted the self-assurance of the guilty king by the pertinent and searching inquiry: "What meaneth then this bleating of the sheep in mine ears, and this lowing of the oxen which I hear?" Saul still attempted a justification of himself. It can hardly be believed that he was thinking much of sacrifice before; he certainly was not now, under the keen rebuke of the prophet, in a very devotional frame. He was probably thinking more how to save himself from the chastisement which he knew he so richly merited. The idea of sacrifice was only the fig-leaf device to hide the nakedness of conscious guilt. Thin as the subterfuge is, however, he is disposed to make the most of it.

Finding now that it will not do to appropriate and use all this booty which he has taken from the Amalekites precisely as he had intended, the thought readily occurs to him, these are precisely the right materials for a sacrifice. He cannot make it useful to himself; suppose he should make one great sacrifice of the whole, and offer it to the Lord, — what a splendid oblation it will make! Will not the Lord be appeased by such a noble offering? Will not the prophet be really taken with such an ostentation of devotion? A capital idea! It will make this spoil an offering in a double sense : first, an offering to his own vanity, and, second, an offering to the Lord. Besides, will not the offering of the spoil in sacrifice fulfil the work that had been left incomplete, and even give it a more beautiful and imposing finish than had originally been designed? And so he tells the prophet that they have brought this spoil from the Amalekites : "for the people spared the best of the sheep and of the oxen, to sacrifice unto the Lord thy God; and the rest we have utterly destroyed." Whereupon the following colloquy ensues : —

"Then Samuel said unto Saul, Stay, and I will tell thee what the Lord hath said to me this night. And he said unto him, Say on. And Samuel said, When thou wast little in thine own sight, wast thou not made the head of the tribes of Israel; and the Lord anointed thee king over Israel? And the Lord sent thee on a journey, and said, Go and utterly destroy the sinners, the Amalekites, and fight against them until they be consumed. Wherefore, then, didst thou not obey the voice of the Lord; but didst fly upon the spoil, and didst evil in the sight of the Lord? And Saul said unto Samuel, Yea, I have obeyed the voice of the Lord, and have gone the way which the Lord sent me, and have brought Agag, the King of Amalek, and have utterly destroyed the Amalekites. But the people took of the spoil, sheep and oxen, the chief of the things that should have been utterly destroyed, to sacrifice unto the Lord thy God in Gilgal. And Samuel said, Hath the Lord as great delight in burnt offerings and sacrifices as in obeying the voice of the Lord? Behold, to obey is better than sacrifice, and to hearken than the fat of rams."

When it is finally announced, at the conclusion of this rebuke, that he is rejected from being king, then does Saul first bethink himself to set earnestly about the business of repentance. He now confesses his transgression, craves the prophet's pardon, and begs him to turn again with him, that he may worship the Lord. But his repentance comes too late. Samuel decidedly refuses, but repeats that the Lord hath rejected him from being king over Israel. As the prophet turned to go away, the coming retribution must have seemed awfully near, and intensely real, to the stricken man. As Samuel turned to go, Saul, in his desperation, laid hold of his mantle, and it rent. "And Samuel said unto him, the Lord hath rent the kingdom of Israel from thee this day, and hath given it to a neighbor of thine that is

better than thou. Also, the Strength of Israel
will not lie, nor repent; for he is not man that
he should repent."

II.

CHARACTER AND PREVALENCE OF THIS ERROR.

The truth is, Saul's last error is worse than
the first. He would therein fully endorse his
first disobedience, and would even invoke God's
endorsement of it also. So far from confessing
his guilt, he would clothe it in all the sanctities
of the highest acts of devotion. Instead of
humbling himself in submission to the divine
authority, and seeking direction from his word,
his was the daring impiety of presuming to
counsel God, and prescribe terms to him. In
short, it was a rebel demanding the rights of
citizenship, because of a new and most high-
handed and atrocious act of rebellion. It was
but an insult and a mockery to thus piece out
his former deficiencies by acts of devotion,
which, before they could in any wise be
accepted, required that the worshipper should be
truly submissive to the divine will, and in the

exercise of an obedient faith. Sacrifices were right in their place, when offered according to the divine prescription; but obedience was, and ever must be, first, and no sturdiest performance of one class of duties can make up for our neglect in another class.

It would seem that so plain a lesson should never have been forgotten; but we shall not have to look far to find melancholy proofs that our sinful race are wonderfully prone to forget it. Departing from the word of God, and then attempting to make good their title to his favor by the regularity with which they attended to the formalities of devotion, was the crying sin of the Israelites from the first. How deep and burning is the indignation with which the prophets denounce the twofold wickedness! And thereby do they show that the evil was fearfully prevalent among the people, throughout the period of the prophetic history. When our Saviour came, he found the Pharisees neglecting the most common obligations which they owed to their fellow-men, and with no aptness to listen to the voice of God, nor inclination to obey him; but, nevertheless, making the most ostentatious display of their devotions, — tithing mint, and anise, and cummin, but neglecting the weightier matters of the law, judgment, mercy, and faith; and binding heavy burdens, and laying them upon men's shoulders, while they made void the commandment · of God by their tradition. What a spectacle of apostasy did that nation present! keeping up, in the pride of imposing ceremonial, the outward semblance of religion after the life of it was gone! A people whose religious life was only of this galvanic type was surely ripening for the approaching doom.

Nor shall we fail to find, strewn thick along the history of the Christian dispensation and church, the sins of which that of the King of Israel is a type, — sins that call loudly for the admonition of the prophet to be lifted up anew. "Behold, to obey is better than sacrifice." There are two classes of these evils, each of which calls for a special notice.

III.

HUMAN DEVICES DISPLACE THE COMMANDMENTS OF GOD.

First in order are those in which the command of God is unheeded, and some human invention is substituted in its place. The apostolic warning, "Let no man spoil you through philosophy and vain deceit, after the traditions of men, after the rudiments of the world, and not after Christ," clearly indicates that thus early this class of evils had become fearfully prevalent, and the tendency to apostatize in that direction had become alarmingly active. The Gospel of John and the First Epistle of John are generally believed to have been written purposely to counteract this tendency, and bring the early disciples back to the simplicity of a gospel obedience. That some of the Pauline epistles were written with this design is too clearly manifest to admit of a doubt. When the voices of the apostles and first teachers of Christianity were heard no longer, this tendency to overlay the obedience

of faith with human devices developed itself
with great rapidity.

Then the Episcopal domination began to
displace the authority of Him who is Head
over all things to the church. The boast of
antiquity which the Episcopacy puts forth it
is not worth while to dispute. Its progress
can be traced through the centuries, in a succession of mitred oppressors, who exercised
a rigorous lordship over God's heritage; in the
bloody track of its cruel and relentless persecutions, and in the manifold corruptions to
which it gave rise in the Christian church.
That succession reaches back at least to very
early, if not to apostolic, times, though holding
no relation whatever to the apostles themselves;
and from those early days to the present time
has never ceased to preach the gospel according to Diotrephes, who loveth the pre-eminence.
As the teachings of Jesus were more and more
set aside, an enslaving ritualism of human
prescription was made to bind the consciences
of men, and a gorgeous and imposing ceremonial
was substituted for the pure worship of Him
who seeketh such to worship him as worship

him in spirit and in truth. It is not too much
to say that this unholy spirit of Antichrist
polluted everything it touched. It laid ir-
reverent hands upon the institutions of the
gospel, whenever and wherever it could, in so
doing, serve the guilty purposes of its lofty
and growing pretensions.

IV.

INFANT BAPTISM. DR. BUSHNELL'S THEORY.

So early as the beginning of the third century
human invention had found a substitute for one
of the positive institutions of the church of
Christ, which has ever since been exceedingly
popular with all who choose to disobey the
King whom God hath set upon his holy hill
of Zion. We refer to infant baptism. Tertullian
is the first Christian writer who mentions it, and
he mentions it only to protest against it, — a
fact which of itself is sufficient to prove its non-
apostolic origin. It is enough to condemn the
practice, in the estimation of any unsophisti-
cated mind, that it does not appear, in so much
as the remotest allusion, in the New Testament
writings, nor in the practice of the apostles.

Add to this, that all the most competent historians and commentators assure us that it had no existence till long after the apostolic age.

Dr. Bushnell has devoted the first half of his work on Christian Nurture to the task of concocting a plausible theory for infant baptism, by which to lift it out of the desuetude into which it has latterly fallen. But his argument is suicidal. He tells us that the faith of the infant is included in that of the parent, and hence the propriety of its baptism. Even if the premises were true, the conclusion does not follow. If the parent's faith includes that of the child, then must it also include all that that faith includes. Among the things included in a true Christian faith is the obedience of faith; and one item of that obedience is baptism. If, then, the parent's faith is to stand for that of the child, why, we ask, in the name of consistency, does not his obedience stand for that of the child also, and consequently his baptism stand for the child's baptism? And the practical conclusion that would legitimately follow would be, that the child of a Christian parent does not need baptism; in fact, that infant baptism is out of place, and manifestly inappropriate.

But the premises are false, as the argument based upon them is self-contradictory. We take it, if any man has faith, he has it to himself, before God; and if any human being obeys God, he obeys for himself, and not for another; as each of us, also, must give account of himself to God. In short, moral obligation is strictly individual and personal. We cannot do another's duties for him. No other person can do ours for us. Let it be borne in mind that baptism is never mentioned in the New Testament except in such terms as imply a conscious subject, and a voluntary obedience. The command to "be baptized" must be addressed to an intelligent, conscious subject. He would justly be regarded as insane who should address such a command to any other. A few grains of common sense will be sufficient, too, to teach any one that such a command can never be obeyed, except by the voluntary act of the person to whom it is addressed. It will be seen, then, that this command of Christ is set aside just so far as infant baptism prevails.

Could there be a more clear and unmistakable instance of "teaching for doctrines the commandments of men," and "making void the commandments of God by human tradition"? Is it not the very error of the King of Israel,— that of supplementing the deficiencies of his obedience by devices of his own? Or, rather, it is the forestalling of Christian obedience by human intervention.

V.

OUR RESPONSIBILITY AS TO THE ORDINANCES OF THE GOSPEL.

Our responsibility as to the ordinances of the gospel is certainly not as well understood as it should be, and certain religious teachers seem not disposed to have it very well understood. There are many who are so accustomed to talk loosely in regard to baptism, to make of it anything or nothing, as their own caprice may dictate, to regard it as a mere punctilio that may be modified to any extent that will suit individual taste or convenience, that they cannot appreciate the position of one who holds himself morally bound to keep the ordinances as they were delivered to us by inspired authority and apostolic teaching and practice. Surely, the first requisite of a sound Christianity is a submissive, obedient spirit. There is a manifest fallacy in the view, and a fearful responsibility incurred in the spirit, that would presume to sit in judgment on matters of divine authority, and set aside, or modify divine decisions.

They who accept this loose view of the case are at great pains to interpret our Saviour's command so indefinitely that it shall specify nothing in particular; and so we are taught that our Saviour has been so unskilful in the use of language, that the law which he has enacted for his church enacts nothing definite; that his most positive comm'and commands nothing positive; and his chosen symbol of descipleship is left without specified form. To attribute such indefiniteness to a human law-giver would be to impeach his wisdom. Is it any less an impeachment of Him who spake as never man spake?

Again, if that which we practise for baptism

is really the ordinance of Christ's appointment, then this one fact puts all criticism in regard to it out of countenance, and all cavils as to convenience or propriety are set aside, as impertinent and out of place. But if it is not of Christ's appointment, but only a human invention, it is itself an impertinence, and is entitled to no more respect than the inventions of heathenism; and he who practises it as an act of Christian consecration is really performing an impious desecration, that, so far from leading himself or others to Christ, is leading them directly away from him; and the very act which professes to declare allegiance to Christ is an act of downright rebellion against him.

It must be evident to every one that baptism could not have originated save in the positive command of Christ. That command alone could define it, establish its proprieties, clothe it with utilities, and give it meaning. If anything else is substituted for the institution of his appointment, then propriety, utility, meaning, all are lost; and we have but a specious cheat, in which a gross deception is palmed off upon the world, while a most solemn act of divine ser-

vice is transformed into a delusion : an acted
falsehood before our fellow-men, a mockery and
a profanation offered up to God.

And what shall we say of the guilt of that administrator who repeats the baptismal formula
over a ceremony that is not the ordinance of
Christ's appointment, — what, but that every
time he says, " I baptize thee," he utters an un-
truth ; and that when he goes on to say, " In the
name of the Father, and the Son, and the Holy
Spirit," he uses the name of the sacred three to
emphasize the falsehood? Before venturing on
the act itself, or any complicity with it, or any
responsibility for it, in which the authority of
God is renounced, the wisdom of the Saviour
impeached, God mocked, our fellow-men de-
ceived, and the ordinances of the church and
the truth of the gospel perverted, — were it not
well for us to pause, and consider whither we
are drifting?

The principle once admitted that we may set
aside, or supplement, or abridge, the divine
testimony, and it will be difficult to fix limits
to its application. It will be found of ample
dimensions to admit the Romish corruptions

and usurpations on the one hand, and the worst perversions of modern rationalism on the other.

VI.

PLAINNESS OF THE CASE TO AN EARNEST INQUIRER.

Let us now suppose that one who is an earnest inquirer after truth, and who, in full sincerity of soul, desires to obey Christ, has this question of baptism under consideration. The whole subject will be found wonderfully simple and plain. He finds, in the first place, that this is a duty which an individual is himself to do. Whatever has been done to him by others, without his option, it is clear cannot be Christian baptism. He will notice, too, that the ordinance is instituted by positive divine command; that is, a command resting solely on divine appointment. All questions of expediency may therefore be dismissed, at once, as wholly irrelevant to the case. The question is now reduced to a very simple form, namely, " What hath God said? " He can eliminate from

6

the inquiry all questions as to what men have said.

He now opens the New Testament at the account of his Saviour's baptism. He would desire, by all means, to have his obedience conform to that of him who "fulfilled all righteousness." He reads of our Saviour's "going down into the water" and being baptized, and then "coming up out of the water." The same mode of representation is made in other cases. Confident that he must find the very act somewhere specified, he pursues his inquiries, steadfastly keeping by the Word of God. Coming to the sixth of Romans, he reads of being "buried" with Christ by baptism, and rising again. In Colossians he finds this language repeated. In one of the epistles to the Corinthians he finds the same form of the ordinance again alluded to. Thus he finds the *form* distinctly specified in the New Testament. No other is mentioned, or even suggested.

He can no longer hesitate as to what constitutes the act of baptism. It is being buried in water and rising from the water. He finds, too, that a meaning is given to the ordinance, that requires this particular form for its expression. Nay, the apostle affirms this particular form to have been chosen purposely that this meaning might be expressed.

He has before him, then, no question of different modes, among which he is to choose, as suits his caprice or convenience. He has no election in the case. It must be this particular thing prescribed and defined in the New Testament, or it is not Christian baptism. He knows, too, that none of the forms which men devise can, by any possibility, express the meaning which baptism was designed to express. For sprinkling and pouring, and that nondescript performance now very much in vogue of merely laying the moistened fingers upon the brow, cannot surely represent a burial; nor can they be accepted as passable substitutes for it. They have not the merit of being respectable counterfeits. He can no longer hesitate. He goes down into the water, and is " buried by baptism into death; that like as Christ was raised from the dead by the glory of the Father, even so " he " should walk in newness of life." He comes up out of the water and goes on his way rejoicing.

His course may seem exclusive to others. It may, in fact, be strait and narrow; but it has that about it which can be experienced in no other way; he can pursue it with the sweet consciousness of the divine approval. He *knows* that he is obeying God; and this to him is of value far above rubies. He can say to those who press him with their substitutes, "Behold, to *obey* is better than sacrifice." "In vain do you teach for doctrines the commandments of men."

> " Should all the forms that men devise
>   Assault my faith with treacherous art,
> · I'd call them vanity and lies,
>   And bind the gospel to my heart."

VII.

ONE CLASS OF DUTIES SUBSTITUTED FOR ANOTHER.

There is yet another class of errors, in which duties are made to change places, and one set of duties are substituted for another. If the error we have been considering has sadly perverted and corrupted the external form, no less do these poison the fountain of piety in the soul, and eat into the life of godliness. They all proceed on the assumption that it is possible for us to exceed our real obligations in a given line of action; and so we are at liberty to place the surplus to the credit of former deficiencies,— a principle which is manifestly false, inasmuch as we are taught, when we have done our best, to say, " We are unprofitable servants ; we have done only what it was our duty to do."

Now take the case of the man who disregards his moral obligations, or at least is conscious of deficiencies therein ; who perchance is wanting in veracity, dishonest in his dealings, impure in conversation, or an evil-speaker, or profane. Is this man to think of purchasing impunity by prayers and watchful vigils? Will any extra diligence in the exercises of devotion make up for his moral delinquencies? Surely not. He is in the gall of bitterness and the bonds of iniquity ; and nothing can restore him to a true position but a sincere repentance, and return to the walks of uprightness. Until this is done his devotions themselves are laden with the burden of his guilt, and are but the offering up of sin.

Reverse this case, and you have the position of the moralist. He will be justified by his good deeds, while he takes little account of anything purely religious. He claims the divine approbation on the simple ground of his own meritoriousness. It is certainly not a promising beginning that he is turning away from all real obedience to God, and so pouring contempt on his authority, and that he will even make his morality itself the basis of this high-handed rebellion. He will practise the moralities towards his fellow-men, but put aside as unworthy of his regard the positive commands of Jehovah, and the deeper and more spiritual obligations which he owes to God. Surely his Creator has the first claims upon him; and the morality that is made to sanction and support his disregard of these claims can hardly be regarded, in the estimation of Heaven, as other than a worthless counterfeit. In the dazzling light of God's countenance, his boasted goodness vanishes like the morning cloud and the early dew. After all

their boastfulness, it is not usually observed
that moralists are really better than humble
Christian people who feel that their only hope
of justification and salvation must be the righteousness of Christ, and who repeat with the
utmost sincerity the publican's prayer, "God be
merciful to me a sinner." It is impossible to
commend good morals too highly; but the
morality loses all title to our praise when it
is insultingly offered up to God as a sacrifice
which is to atone for manifest disobedience.
The moralist is but practising over again the
gross iniquity of Saul, in offering to God a re-
bellious sacrifice.

Again, nothing can be justly considered as of
more importance, in the whole range of religious activities, than the spirit and temper
which we habitually exercise; inasmuch as it is
on the renewal of the spiritual nature that our
meetness for the heavenly inheritance is made
to depend. An error here is a fatal error. It
may carry with it indubitable evidence that we
are deceiving ourselves as to our real position
in the sight of God. Might not our Saviour's
rebuke to his disciples, "Ye know not what

manner of spirit ye are of," often apply with wonderful point and power?

Our duty is not less clear in this respect than it is in regard to the more external forms and modes which Christianity prescribes. Our spiritual kinship with Christ binds us to the cultivation of a spirit kindred with his own. Christ is our spiritual exemplar no less than our external pattern. Hence the industry and perseverance enjoined in cultivating the meekness and gentleness that characterized him. "Let this mind be in you which was also in Christ Jesus." There is no place for a proud, indomitable, selfish, and censorious spirit, or an impatient, fretful, and irascible temper. These belong to the works of the flesh, which are to be crucified, with the affections and lusts. Ah, it is no small matter for us to gain the victory here! It requires constant watchfulness and very persistent fighting to subdue these internal foes and betrayers. Many a one who has stood forth in confident and zealous championship of Christ and the Christian cause has, in these internal conflicts, found himself defeated and discrowned, and the banner of his faith has trailed in the mire of pollution. "Stronger is he that ruleth his own spirit than he that taketh a city."

Now it may be that the thought that other performances are to make up for deficiencies here may not be put into words, or even shape itself into definite forms of thought, and yet it may be all the time tacitly admitted, and acted upon. We need very earnestly to cultivate the spirit and temper of the Master. Even Christian dignity, assurance, and indignation against outward evil need to be tempered with the meekness and gentleness that were in Christ; with long-suffering, forbearance, faith, patience.

> And, by all thy nature's weakness,
>   Hidden faults, and follies known,
> Be thou, in rebuking evil,
>   Conscious of thy own.
>
> Not the less shall stern-eyed Duty
>   To thy lips her trumpet set;
> But with harsher blasts shall mingle
>   Wailings of regret.
>
> So, when thoughts of evil-doers
>   Waken scorn, or hatred move,
> Shall a mournful fellow-feeling
>   Temper all with love.

We might proceed to notice other forms of this error; such as substituting secret prayer for the more social or public duties of religion, or these duties in the stead of private devotion; a neglect of all the more spiritual activities of the religious life, and making up by special attention to business matters; or a total neglect of the outward business of the house of God, to be made up by extra diligence in spiritual operations; a neglect to engage in earnest efforts for the salvation of others, to be made up by an exhibition of the more quiet traits of piety; or a neglect of piety at home, made up by labors for the salvation of others; and the bountiful giving for the cause of Christ that is to atone for all other deficiencies; or the niggardly meanness that either gives nothing at all, or gives as though the Holy City were an extremely unprofitable speculation, but hoping to balance the account by an unnatural ostentation of devoutness.

VIII.

THE WAY OF OBEDIENCE THE ONLY WAY OF SAFETY.

But enough. It will be seen that the commandments of God are exceedingly broad; that they lay their requisitions upon the whole life, and upon every part of it, and claim full control of all our modes of acting and living. It will be seen, too, that the way of obedience is a strait and narrow way. Let me assure you, reader, it is the only way of safety. You remember how Bunyan's pilgrim, footsore and weary, sat down to rest by the side of the way; and while there, that he discovered a path all carpeted with luxuriant green, and overhung by a grateful shade, that seemed to run parallel with the one he was travelling. You remember how he pursued that path, till the shades of twilight enveloped the way, and the twilight deepened into midnight gloom; and then the thunders roared awfully overhead, and the lightnings glanced fearfully, and sounds of evil omen assailed his ear, and shapes of dread

and fearful pitfalls were in the way. You remember his long captivity in Doubting Castle,
and his oft-repeated chastisements by the hand
of Giant Despair. Alas that so sombre a
picture should so often be so fully realized!
Many a disciple has thus left, little by little,
and almost imperceptibly at the first, the simplicity of the gospel, until his way has become
so darkened by sin, and he has become so lost
to truth and goodness, that blow after blow
of heavy chastisement was needed, before he
could be brought back to the obedience of
faith.

Oh, how much better to follow in the Lord's
appointed way, though that way be narrow,
and difficult, and even thorny! It may, indeed,
lead right over the very summit of the Hill
Difficulty, or down into the depths of the
Valley of Humiliation, or even through the
dark Valley of the Shadow of Death. You
may be jeered at and ridiculed by the whole
town of Vanity Fair. Demas, who loveth this
present world, may seek to lead you aside to
some silver mine; or By-Ends, by all deceitful

blandishments of self-righteousness, and allure-
ments of false doctrine, may tempt you astray.
But in addition to such trials of your faith,
you will find springs of living water even in
the desert, and many a "cool retreat" that
shall be to you as "the shadow of a great rock
in a weary land." You may, too, in some
favored hour, be led by friendly hands up the
Delectable Mountains, from whose summits,
your vision cleared from the mists of worldli-
ness, you may catch ravishing glimpses of the
land that is "very far off." Or you may be permitted to walk in the beautiful land of Beulah,
that borders the river of Death, where the
"shining ones" come trooping down from the
pearly gates to give you joyful greeting, and
choral harmonies, uprising from the celestial
battlements, come floating down over the
dark river to your delighted ear and are borne
inward to your soul from the harps of the
City of God.

Then, Christian pilgrim, then will it be seen
that the way of obedience is the only right way,
the only way that is safe; that the slightest

disobedience has danger, and even death, in it; that, therefore, to obey, fully, cheerfully, unhesitatingly to obey, is better, far better, than sacrifice.

IV.

A PROVERB IN ISRAEL.

CHAPTER IV.

A PROVERB IN ISRAEL.

I.

THE PROVERBIAL QUESTION.

HE words in which the people had expressed their astonishment when Saul first prophesied among the prophets, are again recorded in the twenty-fourth verse of the nineteenth chapter of 1 Samuel. In this instance they are introduced with the words "they say;" indicating thus that the saying had now passed into a proverb. "Wherefore they say, Is Saul also among the prophets?" The words are the same; but their suggestive import, and the train of reflections to which they give rise, are very different.

At the first, the question was asked in connection with a wonderful event in the life of Saul. He had just been anointed, though not yet inaugurated king; when, coming to the place where the company of the prophets dwelt, the Spirit of God came upon him, and he prophesied among the prophets. It was nat- ural for the people, knowing as they did the previous obscurity of Saul and of his family, to give utterance to their astonishment by asking "Is Saul also among the prophets?" It was the strangeness of the incident that gave rise to the question. Its import must have been wholly incidental. There could not, from that first event, have arisen that proverbial significance with which it was afterwards invested.

The next nine chapters following the record we have here considered, contain what is left to us of fourteen years of eventful history, in which the moral and political status of the king had become entirely changed, and the kingdom was being molten in the furnace of revolution. Saul seems to have made rapid progress in un- godliness, till his rebellion against the divine authority cost him his kingdom. David had received the divine anointing, as his suc- cessor; and, at the same time, that divine spirit which had been with Saul from the first departed from him and rested upon David. In place of it, an "evil spirit"—a spirit evidently of gloominess and dejection, of remorse and fear — took possession of him, and wrought in him that frame of mind best fitted for the exercise of all evil passions. The jealousy with which he had already begun to regard the rising fortunes of the son of Jesse was fanned into an unquenchable flame of vengeful and relentless hate by the voice of the daughters of Israel, as they met them returning from the wars, and sang, " Saul hath slain his thousands, but David his ten thousands."

An insatiable desire to compass the destruction of God's anointed now became a ruling passion with him. The nineteenth chapter relates how, on one occasion, he sought with his own hand to take his life : " And Saul sought to smite him, even to the wall, with the javelin; but he slipped away out of Saul's presence, and he smote the javelin into the wall. And David fled, and escaped that night." Finding himself still pursued, he made his way to the home of the old prophet in Naioth of Ramah.

II.

HOW IT BECAME PROVERBIAL.

And here it was that the strange events occurred with which the passage quoted is connected, and which give it its special significance : " Saul sent messengers to take David, and when they saw the company of the prophets prophesying, and Samuel standing as appointed over them, the Spirit of God came upon the messengers of Saul, and they prophesied. And when it was told Saul, he sent other messengers, and they prophesied likewise ; and Saul sent messengers the third time, and they prophesied also." Foiled in these repeated attempts, he resolved to take the work into his own hands. He would no longer trust to messengers. He would go himself and destroy the royal fugitive. Full of his guilty purpose, and enraged even to desperation at his former ill-success, he starts upon his wicked errand ; when, lo ! as he approached the home of the prophets, " the Spirit of God was upon him also, and he went on and prophesied, until he came to Naioth of

Ramah." And there, instead of accomplishing his evil design, so completely was he overmastered and controlled by the spirit that was upon him, that he seems entirely to have forgotten it, for the time ; and stripping off his armor and his royal robes, and thus rendering himself completely defenceless, he remained a day and a night among the prophets. His very rage had brought him into a position where he was impelled to deeds and utterances the most distasteful to him. He started to thwart the ends of prophecy, and he finds himself compelled to reaffirm it.

But that a great criminal, full of demoniac fury, bent on the perpetration of the most horrible of crimes, should, by the very infatuation and rage with which he was pursuing his infamous purpose, be suddenly brought to endorse the very cause he opposed, to sanction the course, and, by his own acts, secure the present safety of his intended victim, — this is strange, passing strange. And it was this which gave its proverbial significance to the question which the people were asking each other anew, in mutual astonishment. "Wherefore they say, Is Saul also among the prophets?"

III.

HISTORICAL PARALLELS.

But, strange as these events appear, excepting in the circumstances of miraculous intervention, a little reflection concerning human affairs will discover many an interesting and instructive parallel. Individual instances are scattered all along the pages of history, from the earliest to the most recent times, in which the assailants of Christianity have become unintentionally most veracious witnesses to its truth.

One of the earliest opposers of Christianity, who engaged in a direct attack upon it, was Celsus. He employed all the offensive methods of argument, ridicule, and denunciation, and, no doubt, felt sure, when he had completed his famous work entitled "A True Discourse," that he had utterly demolished the religion he had assailed. But, strange to say, in the very work written expressly for the refutation and entire overthrow of the gospel is found the most striking confirmation of it. While his argument is utterly suicidal, the fact that he constantly refers to the facts recorded in the four gospels as well-known facts, makes his work strongly corroborative of the gospel history, and therefore invaluable to the Christian apologist.

While the writings of Celsus were received with gladness by the enemies of the Christian cause, Christianity moved on steadily to the achievements of its early triumphs; strong in its self-evidencing power, in its consistent appeal to established facts, in the excellence of its teaching, in the heavenly purity of its principles, and the blessed fruits which it everywhere bore. · And Celsus, and Porphyry, and Julian, and other early sceptical writers hold the place which their names now occupy in history, mainly by reason of the use that is made of them by Christian writers in confirmation of the truth they once assailed.

As it happened to these earlier opposers, so has it fared with the sceptical writers of subsequent times. Either by their own self-contradictions, or their refutations of each other, they have scarcely more than reaffirmed the truth they so stoutly denied. No system on earth was ever assailed with such variety and malignity of oppositions as Christianity. No book in existence was ever subjected to so rude and merciless a criticism as the Bible; yet the only result has been to display in bolder relief the royal honors, and manifest supremacy, and resplendent excellence of the Christian system; while archæology and history, the explorations of the antiquarian and the modern traveller, the study of ancient manuscripts and of ancient monuments, — all are constantly bringing fresh contributions to the already ample stock of Christian evidence, and re-affirming with added emphasis the leading facts of Bible history.

IV.

CONTRADICTIONS AND MUTUAL REFUTATIONS OF ERRORISTS.

It is interesting to observe how sceptical theories have been perpetually displacing each other. The cynical little Frenchman who toadied and pilfered at the court of Frederick the Great, and who thought he had actually annihilated the Christian religion by his sneers and grimaces, and the miserable sot who wrote the "Age of Reason," have long ago been set aside, as a long way behind the times. Voltaire and Paine are not even respectable enough to keep company with the gloved and slippered gentry of the modern sceptical school. But the mutual refutations and inherent contradictions of this opposition were never more apparent than in the infidel literature of the present day.

The case is stated with admirable force and accuracy in the following paragraph, quoted from the "Bibliotheca Sacra :" "Scepticism, like some rebel army, has often had its transient jubilee, and made its short-lived panic. But step by step it has abandoned stronghold after stronghold, and seems now to be looking more and more diligently for the last ditch. It stands confessing our main facts, or denying them by principles that are suicidal. The men that push these marauding expeditions stand out but as a fraction and a faction in the world of criticism, whose own sympathizers reciprocally often wash their hands of the folly. Strauss hacks away at Paulus, and some better men; Baur makes Strauss wince; Renan strides over both; Schenkel hints at their disparagement of evidence, and Schenkel's admiring translator spends his chief strength in disputing his inferences and denying his statements." The scene enacted in the palace of the high priest when Christ was put on trial is a type of the trial to which Christianity has been subjected through its whole history. "For many bare false witness against him, but their witness agreed not together; and there arose certain and bare false witness against him," uniting their testimony on one distinct specification. "But neither so did their witness agree together."

It is surely a significant fact, that the sceptics of the present day busy themselves chiefly in writing lives of Jesus, thus admitting the main facts of Christianity, while attempting to resolve its particulars into shadowy myth. As with Saul when in wrathfulness he went forth to destroy the youthful king of Israel, so has it

ever been when a spirit like that of Saul has
attempted the destruction of David's greater
Son. "Wherefore, they say, Is Saul also among
the prophets?"

v.

OUTWARD OPPOSITION. — JULIAN AND OTHER OPPOSERS.

And when from argument opposition has
proceeded to overt acts, it has met with no
more prosperous results. The Emperor Julian,
in the fourth century, determined on the defeat
of the Christian cause and the extinction of the
Christian name. He persecuted the Christians,
denied them the privilege of professing their
faith, robbed their churches and closed them
against the Christian worship, and sought to
reinstate the Pagan worship in all its ancient
splendor. And finally, in order to refute the
prophecy of Christ in regard to the temple at
Jerusalem, he attempted to have it rebuilt.
Against this attempt the powers of nature
seemed leagued in jealous opposition; for
subterranean fires are said to have burst forth

repeatedly and scattered and terrified the work-
men, so that the work could not proceed ; and
the enterprise had finally to be abandoned.
Foiled in all his efforts, he fell at length mortally
wounded while conducting a war against the
Persians.   Finding his life fast ebbing away,
the once haughty emperor, now humbled at the
near approach of death, lifted his dying gaze
to the bending heavens above him, and ex-
claimed, "O Galilean ! thou hast conquered."
Yes ! Julian, yes ! The Galilean evermore
conquers, and with a sovereignty greater than
all that is crowned with royal diadems rides
forth conquering and to conquer.   And the
maddened spirit of Saul in the very acme of
deadliest hostility shall evermore be compelled
to prophesy among the prophets.   "He hath
upon His vesture and upon His thigh a name
written, King of kings and Lord of lords."

Of modern illustrations none will more readily
occur, or be more frequently cited, than that
of the class of politicians who bore sway in this
country at the outbreak of our recent war.   It
is not difficult to trace in their history a striking parallel with that of the first king of Israel.

After enjoying a supremacy that afforded the noblest opportunities, like him they were compelled to see that power passing into other hands. Like him, they had forfeited that power by their ungodliness and want of moral principle. Like him, they became irritated, more and more, because of the futility of the efforts which they put forth for its recovery. Like his, too, their methods became those of madness; and in that madness they were led to the utterance and vindication of truths they had all their lives combated both in word and deed. "Wherefore they say, Is Saul also among the prophets?"

VI.

A MORAL PROVIDENCE.

Now it is manifest that these things come to pass not by chance, but by the operation of a general law, a moral providence in this world that has appointed bounds and measures to the existing evil, which it cannot pass. So that falsehood, grown furious in its assaults upon truth, becomes self-contradictory; and wrong, pushed recklessly to an extreme, becomes self-destructive; and they who madly rush against Jehovah's buckler do but destroy themselves.

When evil is put upon its own defence, when it is compelled to the work of self-assertion, it thereby discloses its native enormity, reveals its inherent weakness, and thence results its overthrow. The waves begin to foam and rage as they approach the shore. But just there, too, are they met by a strong undertow, by which their power is overthrown and utterly annihilated. So it is in their direct assaults upon the solid ground of truth and right that falsehood and wrong grow wrathful and clamorous; and just there it is that they are rolled back upon themselves in hopeless impotence, and the good cause acquires added strength and security by the trial through which it has passed. When evil men become enraged, and employ the weapons of malice and license, they prepare for themselves a speedy discomfiture. When Satan comes down in great wrath, it is because he "knoweth that he hath but a short time."

The Psalmist recognizes the moral providence

which we are illustrating, and thus anticipates
its operation in the case of his assailants :
" Hide me from the secret counsel of the
wicked, from the insurrection of the workers
of iniquity, who whet their tongue like a sword
and bend their bows to shoot their arrows, even
bitter words, that they may shoot in secret at
the perfect; suddenly do they shoot at him
and fear not. They encourage themselves in
an evil matter. But God shall shoot at them
with an arrow, suddenly shall they be wounded.
So shall they make their own tongue to fall
upon themselves." "Behold! he travaileth
with iniquity and hath conceived mischief and
brought forth falsehood. He made a pit and
digged it, and is fallen into the ditch which he
made. His mischief shall return upon his own
head, his violent dealings shall come down
upon his own pate."

This law has played an important part in history, and has received a fresh illustration in
every important crisis of human affairs. Did
not the hardness of heart, and the wrath of
Pharaoh and his host, drive them headlong to
destruction? And did not the means he

employed for the purposes of oppression secure deliverance to an oppressed but too timorous people? And when they went forth to prevent the exodus of Israel, did they not, instead, actually drive them out, and compel their emancipation? And have we not seen the same thing done, on a grander scale, in our own times? Saul, brought by his wrathfulness to prophesy among the prophets, was it not a type of what took place in the history of his times? The settled malignity of purpose which he pursued towards David, did it not at length drive him upon his own destruction? And did it not at the same time set off the more strikingly, and bring more prominently into notice, the many excellences of head and heart which characterized the youthful Bethlehemite,—his wisdom and prudence, his bravery and magnanimity, his gentleness and benignity? And when they saw the clouded and sullen brow, and all the natural and acquired repulsiveness of the one, and the as yet unsullied honor, joined with the youth and beauty, of the other, think you the daughters of Israel grew less jubilant with their timbrels and dances as they repeated the familiar song : " Saul hath slain his thousands, but David his ten thousands "? Would not the sympathies of the people necessarily be enlisted strongly with the royal fugitive, and against his royal persecutor? And so Saul was securing the very end he sought to prevent, by the very efforts he put forth to prevent it. He was at once paving the way to his own perdition, and that to the exaltation and enthronement of his successor. And so it ever is. When the enemy comes in like a flood, the Spirit of the Lord lifts up a standard against him. The wrath of the persecutor reacts against himself, and " the blood of the martyrs is the seed of the church."

VII.

CONSERVATISM AND PROGRESS.

Saul is a representative of that senile conservatism that clings to the old simply because it is old; though the verdict of Heaven stands recorded that it has forfeited its right to be. David represents the spirit of progress, that takes its rise in the word of God, " in whom

18

was Life, and the Life was the light of men."
An elemental war between them has been continued through the ages, and is destined to continue, till the final conflict and decision of the
great battle-field of Armageddon.

There has never been a useful reform, moral,
social, political, or religious, that has not cost
a struggle between these opposing forces. The
old does not quietly give way when its time
has come, and depart in peace. It resists the
incoming of the new. So it is in the individual. The new birth does not at once create
all things new. The new man is strenuously
resisted by the old; and in some cases, it
would seem, the old man has perpetual predom-
inance,

> " . . . . There are many, even,
> Whose names are written in the Christian Church,
>   . . . . that diet still on mud,
> And splash the altars with it; you might think
> The clay Christ laid upon their eyelids, when,
> Still blind, he called them to the use of sight,
> Remained there, to retard its exercise
> With clogging incrustations."

So, too, it is in society. No sooner is a new

life implanted therein, than conservatism seeks
to arrest its development, by hedging it in
with its body of death.   Turbulent eras in human history have not been produced by the
spirit of progress that is in the world, but by
the resistance that has been made against it.
The stream that is unimpeded in its flow runs
quietly, and without agitation.   It is the obsta-
cle that resists progress that causes turbulence.
The conservative sees the stream quietly mov-
ing past the position he occupies, and, like a
drunken man, he thinks the foundations of the
earth are out of place ; and therefore he franti-
cally cries, "Hold!" as if his simple voice
could remand the waters back to their original
springs in the everlasting hills.   Grown desperate at length, because unheeded, he rushes
madly into the stream, and proceeds to build
barriers across it of his constituted pride,
and wickedness, and impotence, and folly.
But he finds, in the long run, that it is all in
vain.   His efforts, instead of arresting, only
delay a little, and thereby give irresistible
momentum to the spirit of progress.

> What voice can bid the progress stay
> Of Truth's triumphal car?
> What voice arrest the growing day,
> Or quench the solar star?

Let conservatism pile up its barriers, high and hard as the cliffs of Niagara, the waters will rise to the height, and overleap it. Instead of stopping the current, a catastrophe is precipitated, and ever and anon huge masses of the old wickedness are rent away, and plunged out of sight in the abyss below. It is to be expected of a mere partisan that he will cling persistently to his party till every plank of the old ship is turned to rottenness; and that a mere sectarist will cling to his creed until all that gives it distinction is its falsehood. But the desperation with which they cling serves to expose the unsoundness of the one, and the untruthfulness of the other, while the truth and righteousness to which they stand opposed are called into notice thereby.

The desperation with which the Church of Rome, in the sixteenth century, clung to her every superstition; the efforts she put forth to build up her gigantic system of fraud and crime ; the methods of falsehood and corruption which she employed, by which she sought to bind down the nations under her mantle of darkness and ignorance,—all contributed to pave the way for the Reformation, and to ensure its success. All thinking minds were thus compelled to feel the need of it. They were therefore the better prepared to appreciate the purity and glory that irradiated the doctrine of Christ and him crucified. Multitudes, therefore, hailed with joy the new doctrines, and the new order of things they brought with them. Luther, and Calvin, and Zwingle preached, and rested their cause in the power of truth above. To the sturdy blows they dealt to the Romish usurpations, the Vatican rung with empty thunders of excommunication ; but, amid these denunciations and the subsequent persecutions, the word continued to grow, and converts were multiplied.

VIII.

A HOSTILITY ENCOUNTERED BY OUR SAVIOUR.

But we must not omit the illustration of this subject afforded by the history of our Saviour himself.   Never was Christianity assailed with such virulence and variety of opposition as in the person of its Founder.   The powers of this world, the hosts of wicked men, and the powers of darkness, — all led by the prince of the spirits of perdition, and all together bending their multiplied energies, with malignant hate, to the one work of contesting his power, disputing his claims, and preventing the accomplishment of his redemptive work.   And how obviously did all these efforts contribute to the demonstration of his power, to the confirmation of his pre-eminent claims, and the prosperous advancement of his glorious work !   All his enemies did their mightiest against him, and failed ; and thus demonstrated his eternal power and godhead.

All the powers of the kingdom of evil were stirred up in wrath against him to the utter-

most; but the Redeemer pursued his work as
steadfastly, and as little moved, as if no assault
had been made upon him; and thereby was
demonstrated the impotence of the evil powers
to prevail against the kingdom he was estab-
lishing in the world. The temptation served to
show his incorruptibility. Calumny but proved
his innocence; and the attempt to betray him
into folly only made his wisdom the more
apparent. The sufferings to which he was subjected served to reveal in him infinite resources of spiritual strength; while his death
just proved that death had no dominion over
him; and all contributed to show him conqueror, and more than conqueror, leading captivity captive, and receiving gifts for men.

The inspired writers, as they relate the
doings of wicked men against him, are careful
to record that these things came to pass "that
the scripture might be fulfilled." And here
the marvel of Saul among the prophets is all
outdone by the greater wonder, of Satan and
his hosts, both human and demoniac, in their
wrathfulness securing the fulfilment of prophecy and the establishment of the gospel. Wit-

ness that last great trial that concluded the earthly ministry of the Word made flesh. All the concentrated malignity of men and devils assailed him. It was their "hour and the power of darkness." His soul was agonized with draughts of untold bitterness; while, without, the congregated wickedness of men exhausted upon him the arts of cruelty. And yet these evil agents were, all the time, accomplishing the ends of prophecy. The minutest specifications are fulfilled to the very letter.

We notice, especially, the betrayal and the thirty pieces of silver, the mock-trial, the shame, the scourge, the pierced side, the vinegar and the gall, the dividing of the raiment, and casting lots upon his vesture. All that is done to disprove only establishes his Messiahship; all that is done against him but demonstrates the truth of his saying, ". All power is given unto me, both in heaven and on earth;" all that is done to hinder his glorious work only ensures its progress.

IX.

THE SUPREME AUTHORITY.

And his is the authority that rules among
the children of men; that holds the reins of
that redemptive providence in human affairs
which we have briefly traced; by which the
counsels of wickedness are brought to naught,
and its workings are inverted; by which Saul
is compelled to prophesy among the prophets;
and which wrests the utterance of truth and
righteousness even from the slanderous tongues
of their assailants. The evil agent means it for
evil; but God ordains that it shall result in
good.

As we have seen, instances are not wanting,
in the ordinary course of the world, in which
errorists have been compelled, in self-defence,
to acknowledge the truth; in which wrong-
doing has culminated in defence and support of
the right; in which high-handed crime has but
witnessed, and rendered more secure, the innocence it assailed; in which the very infatuation with which a vicious course was pursued has

resulted in the triumph of virtue ; in which lawlessness and violence have made for the establishment of order and law ; and even the wrath of man, that worketh not the righteousness of God, has nevertheless been made to praise him, while the remainder of wrath he has restrained.

The great lesson of all, then, is, that GOD REIGNS, and that the evil in this world is circumscribed within his all-provident control ; and that he will accomplish his purposes, and have his work done, by evil agencies if not otherwise ; for "He doeth according to his will among the hosts of heaven, and among the inhabitants of earth." "THE LORD REIGNETH, LET THE EARTH REJOICE."

V.

FRUITLESS SUPPLICATION.

CHAPTER V.

FRUITLESS SUPPLICATION.

I.

SAUL RESORTS TO PRAYER.

LAST scene of all in this sad, eventful history: Saul, in the posture of a supplicant, uttering the language of earnest prayer. But the heavens are as brass and the earth as iron. There is no penetrating the darkness with which his soul is insphered; and the "great, watchful heavens" look down upon the petitioner in silent scorn. "He that sitteth in the heavens shall laugh; the Lord shall have them in derision." "And when Saul inquired of the Lord, the Lord answered him not, neither by dreams, nor by Urim, nor by prophets."

- These words paint, as by one bold masterstroke, the background of the closing scene in the life of the first king of Israel. No language

125

could depict more graphically the condition
of a soul bereft of all moral and spiritual guidance. He gropes in darkness, and calls for
divine direction, and seeks for light in vain.
The good Spirit of God that had been given
him has been withdrawn. The divine counsel
that had often been given, only to be disregarded, is now withheld. For his disobedience,
his high-handed treason against the God of
Israel, he has been rejected from being king.
He is no longer the true head of the theocratic
government, though still retaining the place,
and exercising the functions of sovereignty.
God has chosen, for that sovereignty, " a man
after his own heart." But this man, hated of
Saul, with a causeless but bitter and cruel
hatred, and hunted as a fugitive from place to
place, has found a refuge from his persecutor,
at length, in the camp of the enemies of Israel.
On a former occasion, in a time of imminent
peril, he had been the savior of Israel. Saul
had now put it beyond his power to obtain help
from that quarter, if indeed he had desired to *
do so.

Besides, his old friend and prophetic counsellor had long since passed away. The mournful record tells us, "Now Samuel was dead; and Israel had lamented him, and buried him in Ramah, even in his own city." And so the last ray of hope is extinguished; and Saul stands before us, gloomy and dejected, a self-ruined and God-forsaken man; just on the eve of a terrible emergency, that might well tax the resources of the holiest, the courage of the bravest, and the wisdom of the wisest. A formidable invasion was on foot. "It came to pass, in those days, that the Philistines gathered their armies for warfare, to fight with Israel. And the Philistines gathered themselves together, and came and pitched in Shunem; and Saul gathered all Israel together, and they pitched in Gilboa." And so the two armies confronted each other. It was evident that mighty events were on the wing. The next few hours might decide the fate of the king and of the kingdom. He cannot remain inactive, and yet he does not know how to act. He is impelled onward, by inexorable necessity, but without the possibility of knowing whither.

Those are awful moments when a soul stands
thus perplexed with infinite contingencies, the
moral atmosphere he breathes all fetid with
the exhalations of former crimes, doomed by
his own free choice to fix his destiny, without
one ray of light to guide him in the choice.
The chances are numberless, that, in his doubt,
and dread, and desperation, he will not act
wisely.

> Stern is the onlook of Necessity.
> Not without shuddering may a human hand
> Grasp the mysterious urn of Destiny.

In ancient times, God sometimes communicated with men, and made known his purposes
to them, or gave them preintimations of the
coming good or evil in dreams. He sent his
angels down through the silence, to anoint the
sleeper with holy unction, and weave into his
dreams the messages of heavenly inspiration.
But how can good angels visit a mind preoc-
cupied with remorseful images of former guilt
and gloomy apprehensions of swift-coming retri-
butions, whose appalling forms fill up the dis-
tempered imagination? There is no avenue

through which the Holiest can come to such a soul, unless he comes to judgment. And so, when Saul inquired of the Lord, he answered him not by dreams.

Another way which God communicated with his chosen people was by Urim and Thummim. Of this method little is known; but it is probable that the divine response was somehow given in connection with the twelve polished jewels that adorned the breast-plate of the high priest. Saul now directs his inquiries towards this oracle, but no response is received — the oracle is silent.

There remained, then, as a last resort, the prophets. Whether they would deign to hold converse with him, after so many warnings had been disregarded, and he had hardened himself against so many reproofs, may well be doubted. At all events, it was rendered certain that they had no divine message for him. Was it not a proverb in Israel, "He that, being often reproved, hardeneth his neck, shall suddenly be destroyed, and that without remedy"? And so, when Saul inquired of the Lord, the Lord

9

answered him not; neither by dreams, nor by
Urim, nor by prophets.

II.

THE CLOSING SCENE IN A GUILTY CAREER.

Finding that God was utterly departed from
him, he forthwith presses his inquiries in
precisely the opposite quarter. Making his
way out of camp in disguise, and under cover
of the darkness, he hastens to consult the
enchantress of Endor. Affrighted at her diabolical disclosures, he returns to the army,
weary, weak, and dispirited : in precisely the
condition to ensure his defeat in the succeeding
conflict. The next day the battle was joined;
and Israel made but a feeble resistance against
the hosts of the Philistines. The army of
Gilboa was trampled down by the invader, or
swept away in the storm of battle, like chaff
of the summer threshing-floor. " And the battle went sore against Saul; and the archers hit
him, and he was sore wounded of the archers.
Then said Saul unto his armor-bearer, Draw
thy sword and thrust me through therewith,

lest these uncircumcised come, and thrust me through, and abuse me. But his armor-bearer would not; for he was sore afraid: therefore Saul took a sword, and fell upon it. And when his armor-bearer saw that Saul was dead, he fell likewise upon his sword, and died with him. So Saul died, and his three sons, and his armor-bearer, and all his men that same day together."

III.

SCRIPTURE RECORD OF HIS SIN.

The chronicler of Israel concludes his account of these events with this brief comment. "So Saul died for his transgressions which he committed against the Lord, even against the word of the Lord, which he kept not; and also for asking counsel of one that had a familiar spirit, to inquire of it, and inquired not of the Lord: therefore he slew him, and turned the kingdom to David, the son of Jesse."

These words lift the veil from any mystery that might otherwise hang over the closing days of this royal sinner's career. He died for his transgressions, we are told. And this transgression was twofold : First, against the Word of the Lord, which he kept not, and, secondly, consulting one who had a familiar spirit, to inquire of it, and not of the Lord. In other words, turning away in rebellion from God, and seeking light in the kingdom and from the prince of darkness.

The prophet, when he anointed him, had pressed upon the attention of both him and his people, in a somewhat extended address, the condition on which the kingdom was established : "If ye will obey the voice of the Lord and serve him, and not rebel against the commandment of the Lord, then shall both ye and also the king that reigneth over you continue, following the Lord your God. But if ye will not obey the voice of the Lord, then shall the hand of the Lord be against you as it was against your fathers." This admonition is enforced with all the power of inspiration, and repeated with affectionate urgency at the close of his address : " As for me, God forbid that I should sin against the Lord in ceasing to pray for you ; but I will teach you the good and the right way. Only fear the Lord, and serve him in truth with all your heart; for consider how great things he hath done for you. But if ye shall still do wickedly, ye shall be consumed, both ye and your king." Such was the condition upon which the people received their king. Such was the condition upon which he received the kingdom.

Scarcely had his rule become established, when an occasion presented itself that furnished a practical test of the king's fidelity to this principle; and, strange to say, thus early was he weighed in the balances and found wanting. He is told thereupon that his kingdom shall not continue, but that the Lord hath chosen him a man after his own heart. Then there follows his great sin in relation to the Amalekites, in connection with which he is plainly told," Because thou hast rejected the word of the Lord, he hath also rejected thee from being king over Israel." His prophet guide now leaves him, and visits him no more. And it is said the Lord repented that he had made him king over Israel.

The very next chapter tells us of the

anointing of David, and also that the Spirit of
the Lord came upon David from that day forward. "But the Spirit of the Lord departed
from Saul, and an evil spirit from the Lord
troubled him." It is evident that from this
time forward there was a power operating upon
his mind that would not let him rest; that pre-
vented him from sinking into apathy and indifference, and that compelled him to feel
continually the goadings of a troubled conscience. Jealousy of David, whom he now
regarded as a rival, combined with his fears to
fill him with the most diabolical passions. His
subsequent career is one continual rebellion
against God and persistent effort to secure the
destruction of this rival. There were brief
periods when there seemed to come upon him
a sense of better things; when he would even
confess his sin and promise amendment; but
never was the confession attended with a hearty
repentance. Scarcely had the words escaped
his lips when the old madness would return:
the vulture still had its beak in his heart.

IV.

AN OLD LESSON ILLUSTRATED.

It is the old lesson illustrated, that the sinner's rejection of God results in his being ultimately rejected of him; that continual disobedience results in moral blindness and infatuation and the ultimate loss of the soul; that he who turns away from the divine light when it is given, may find himself in some desperate emergency calling for that light in vain. "Because I have called and ye refused; I have stretched out my hand and no man regarded, I also will laugh at your calamity, I will mock when your fear cometh. When your fear cometh as desolation, and your destruction cometh as a whirlwind; when distress and anguish cometh upon you, then shall they call upon me, but I will not answer; they shall seek me early, but they shall not find me."

In this view Saul's is no isolated case. The moral ingredients are the same as those in the case of every impenitent sinner. He sinned more conspicuously, and went to perdition in

a royal way. The common sinner none the
less signally rebels against God, involves himself in as palpable a darkness, and makes his
way to a destruction equally swift and sure.
Only take away the kingly trappings and circumstances of royalty, and Saul's is the common
case.

V.

CONSEQUENCES FROM NEGLECT OF RELIGIOUS OPPORTUNITIES.

Let us, then, notice some particulars which
this parallel suggests.

1. There was a time in his life when a noble
destiny was within his reach; when he was
wrought upon by holy impulses; when the
Spirit of the Lord was upon him, and another
heart was given him, and his voice was attuned
to inspiration, and it was said in Israel, "Is
Saul also among the prophets?" So it is with the
dullest and most prosaic, the commonest and
most obscure. There are times when they feel
themselves lifted up, they know not how, to a
higher plane than that of their every-day life;
when another heart is given them, and they

are inspired with loftier aspirations. As when the mariner, lifted to the crest of some huge billow, suddenly has his horizon enlarged and catches a view of headlands that otherwise remain unseen; so are our moral and spiritual natures lifted, as by some under-heaving pressure, into larger views and discoveries of what we are, and what we may be. Then the sinner thinks of God and immortality, of the soul and its salvation, of the Saviour and his need of him, and perchance is almost persuaded to be a Christian. The moment is propitious. The occasion is full of promise. Will he choose the course indicated by the loftier and clearer view, or will he let the occasion pass without reaping one advantage? If one will not decide for the better part when he sees it within his grasp, when the sunlight of heaven is shining upon his way, and his attention is specially directed to a nobler destiny, when will he? Will he be more likely to give a right decision amid the deeper darkness that must succeed, when the light is taken away, when his conscience has become seared, his moral sensibilities blunted, and his whole nature chilled with a frigid indifference? There is an analogy all but perfect between the natural and the spiritual in this respect.

> "There is a tide in the affairs of men,
>   Which, taken at the flood, leads on to fortune;
>   Omitted, all the voyage of their life
>   Is bound in shallows, and in miseries."

"There has been some moment," says Maurice, "some one fleeting moment, in the life of every man, even the most thoughtless, when he has had dreams of better things; when he has heard the voices of the prophets with their harp and their tabret coming down the hill; when he has joined their company and has caught their strains. ·There may have been a time when it has been said of him, ' What! is he, too, among the prophets? Has he found that life is real, and that it is not to go out in miserable efforts for self-advancement, or in more miserable efforts for self-indulgence; that it is to be consecrated to the· service of God and man? That hour, that moment, was *the* hour, *the* moment, of their life, friend and brother. To that God would raise and assimilate the whole of it. Oh, do not let the sluggish, turbid current of your ordinary days seem to you that which truly represents to you what you are, what you are destined to be. No; the time when you made the holiest resolutions; when you struggled most with the powers of evil; when you said it should not be your master; when love conquered you and freed you from other chains that you might wear her chains, — *that*, THAT was the true index to the divine purpose concerning you; that tells you what the Spirit of God is working in you that you may be. You may not be able to revive the feeling which you had then; but He who gave you the feeling, He is with you, is striving with you that you may will and do of his good pleasure. Only do not strive with Him, that He may leave you to yourself and to the power of evil."

2. The time of noblest promise with Saul was in his youth; and this is commonly the case. Childhood and youth is the seed-time; the rest of life is but the growth of what was planted then, and eternity will witness the full maturity and the final harvest. Not only

is the mind more impressible then, but the im-
pressions made produce lasting effects, and
operate with controlling power in after life.   It
is Wisdom herself who gives the admonition,
"Remember thy Creator in the days of thy
youth." What language can fully set forth
the improvidence that would recklessly forfeit
all these advantages and opportunities, contin-
uing to procrastinate, till the " evil days come "!
Many a one who has done so has been compelled
at length to drink a bitter cup, to lie down in
sorrow at the last, exclaiming, " The harvest is
past, the summer is ended, and we are not
saved."

3. Again, the propitious time with Saul was
when he was called to enter upon his life-work ;
when he was first invested with the attribute
of sovereignty.   There is such a period, too,
in the history of every thoughtful person.
When a youth is first wakened to the consciousness of the responsibilities of life resting upon
him ; when he is made to feel that the great
world is before him as the theatre whereon he
is to work out his destiny ; that he must adopt
his calling, and make his way thenceforth by

his own exertions, — then life seems real. The
past illusions no longer satisfy. He can no
longer walk in a vain show. The soul craves
something substantial. How natural that a
sense of responsibility should quicken the whole
moral nature, should open the heavens to the
soul and lead to a sense of God! How many
have found that time of their lives the time
when they were called with a heavenly calling
to the work of faith, to the service of Christ!
How many, too, who have refused to obey that
call, have found all subsequent awakenings
less and less potent to save, till the Spirit of
God has finally been known to them only as
a spirit of remorse and fear, — "an evil spirit
from the Lord," that troubled them.

4. Again, the time when the spirit of prophecy came upon Saul was when he was among
the prophets. Great is the power of human
sympathy. The power of God unto salvation
operates along the lines of social contact. The
divine life is propagated from heart to heart.
The Son of God clothed himself in human
flesh that he might reach us through that
medium. The Holy Spirit on the day of Pen-

tecost was poured out where the disciples
were all gathered together, with one accord, in
one place, and filled the place where they were
sitting. Such is the ordinary method of grace.
For this purpose the church was organized. For
this reason the social institutions of the church
exist. He who finds himself in company with
the disciples, wrought upon by a spirit kindred
with theirs, when the religious interest that is
in their hearts passes over as a heavenly con-
tagion into his, so that he feels impelled to
seek their company, to adopt their language,
and join in their work, stands upon a high
vantage-ground, occupies a position of the
loftiest promise. To lose that vantage-ground,
to shut away from the soul the light of holy
promise, to sink again into apathy and indifference, is to peril all his immortal interests.

5. While it is true in general that every
individual who lives under the light of the
gospel realizes his times of special awakening,
when he feels himself called of God with a
special calling, we also remark that no advantages, however great, or however various, can
ensure his salvation. These advantages in-

crease his responsibilities, but give him no immunities. The best traits of character are no proofs against the possible inroads of vice. Religious influences around us, or resting with power upon our souls, do not make it certain that we shall not be lost at last. God gives us our advantages, and thereby places responsibility in our hands; and then all depends upon what use we make of them. Though one start with every possible advantage, it is by his own agility that he must win the race. Though clad in kingly armor, it is with sturdy blows of his own right hand that he is to conquer.

Witness Saul: once among the prophets; all things around him, all things that were acting upon him, seemingly conspiring to his moral and spiritual elevation. Behold him now, every door of hope closed against him; God maintaining towards him a portentous silence; his soul enveloped in the very midnight of spiritual darkness, and in his desperation seeking the companionship and counsel of the spirits of perdition. Oh, it is a picture drawn from real life of a lost soul, already robed in

the very drapery of hell. O Lucifer! How
art thou fallen, son of the morning!

VI.

PROGRESSIVE DEGRADATION OF CHARACTER.

6. Such moral intervals, be it observed, are
not often passed over at a single leap. Satan
is at great pains to grade the road to hell to
suit each individual's case. Were it not so, he
could not be so deplorably successful. They
who go down the broad way sink gradually,
and by almost imperceptible degrees. We
need therefore to guard the more cautiously
against the first beginnings of evil. It is
hazardous to dally with temptation, to stand
faltering and hesitating, when God clearly
points out the way; to say "if," and "but,"
where God makes all bright with certainties.

You look with disgust upon the confirmed
inebriate; but let me tell you, young man, all
that depth of ruin was involved in the first
draught of the maddening beverage. That
guilty creature whom the daughters of respect-
ability and refinement would shrink from as

from the touch of contamination, whose door
is the way to death, and whose steps take hold
on hell, commenced her career of shame by
simple indiscretions. That villain, whom nobody will trust, commenced with little, scarce
perceptible peccadilloes. That liar, whom nobody
will believe, began, perchance, by slightly add-
ing to or subtracting from the sum total of
the current tattle. Oh, it is the little foxes
that spoil the vines ! Have a care, then ; exercise
a scrupulous vigilance about the beginnings of
sin. The sinner goes down by easy gradations,
his way darkened more and more, till at length
he finds himself " holden with the cords of his
sins, and he shall die without instruction, and
in the greatness of his folly he shall go
astray."

It is the same with religious doubt and disobedience. He who fails to submit to the
claims of God when they are made known to
him, who puts God off for his own convenience,
is entering upon a course that may lead him
to ruinous apostasy at the last ; and he who,
instead of searching for the truth as for hidden
treasure, and seeking to be rooted and grounded

therein, readily entertains and toys with every passing doubt, may find his perceptions darkened more and more, till he loses the power of assured belief. Nay, how often do such persons pass directly over to the opposite side of sceptical credulity, — a position that has, if possible, even less of sound intelligence to recommend it than the grossest superstition. One of the greatest marvels of modern spiritualism is, the facility with which certain minds can turn away from the well-attested truths of the gospel, professing themselves too incredulous to receive the Word of God, and accept forthwith, with the extreme of unreasoning credulity, the vapid, and silly, and senseless outgivings of " one who hath a familiar spirit."

" Speculations," says Mansel, " which end in unbelief, are often commenced in a believing spirit. It is painful, but at the same time instructive, to trace the gradual progress by which an unstable disciple often tears off, strip by strip, the wedding garment of his faith, scarce conscious the while of his own increasing nakedness ; and to mark how the language of Christian belief may remain almost untouched when the substance and the life have departed from it. While philosophy speaks nothing but Christianity, we may be tempted to think that the two are really one; that our own speculations are leading us to Christ by another and a more excellent way. Many a young aspirant after a philosophical faith trusts himself to the trackless ocean of rationalism in the spirit of the too confident apostle: 'Lord, bid me come to thee on the water.' And for a while he knows not how deep he sinks, till the treacherous surface on which he treads is yielding on every side, and the dark abyss of utter unbelief is yawning to swallow him up. Well is it with those who, even in that last fearful hour, can yet cry, 'Lord, save me!' and can feel that supporting hand stretched out to grasp them, and hear that voice so warning, yet so comforting, 'O thou of little faith, wherefore didst thou doubt?' But who that enters upon this course of mistrust shall dare to say that such shall be the end of it? Far better is it to learn, at the outset, the nature of that unstable surface on which we tread, without being tempted by the phantom of religious promise which hangs delusively over it."

VII.

FINAL LOSS OF THE SOUL.

We will not dwell on the sad spectacle of the final wreck and ruin of the soul. Apostasy utter and irremediable; the intellect blinded to all spiritual good; the moral perceptions involved in inextricable confusion; the light of God's countenance utterly and forever withdrawn; and the conscience stung by the scorpion remorse, or tortured with gloomy forebodings. Every one can see how it is possible that a soul may be wakened to the full consciousness of such a state, and at the same time, and by the same means, to the equally full and clear consciousness that there is thenceforth no deliverance from it; that the soul is lost, irrecoverably, forever lost. There is a darkness penetrated by no ray from above; a spiritual death, whose deep Gehenna is never stirred by the power of resurrection; a realm of moral guilt and woe in which divine grace is unknown, and from which recovery is impossible. "There is a sin unto death," — a sin for which there is no intercession. Avoid it. Oh avoid it while you may. "Seek ye the Lord while he may be found; call ye upon him while he is near. Let the wicked forsake his way, and the unrighteous man his thoughts; and let him turn unto the Lord, who will have mercy upon him, and to our God, who will abundantly pardon."

THE END.